You Can Draw

Construction

Illustrated by Ted Williams

Publications International, Ltd.

Cover and interior illustrations by Ted Williams

Text by Amy E. Williams

Louis Weber, CEO
Publications International, Ltd.
7373 North Cicero Avenue
Lincolnwood, Illinois 60712

Permission is never granted for commercial purposes.

Manufactured in China.

8 7 6 5 4 3 2 1

ISBN: 0-7853-8302-6

Contents

How to Draw Construction Vehicles

Drawing can be fun, and it is not as hard as you may think. One of the secrets of drawing is that any object can be broken down into its smaller parts. By following the step-by-step instructions in this book, you can use this secret to learn to draw many different kinds of construction vehicles. By copying these construction vehicles, you will learn basic drawing skills. You will be able to use those skills to draw other objects.

Before you begin, there are some basic tools you need. Make sure you have a pencil, a pencil sharpener, an eraser, a ruler, a felt-tip pen, and of course the grid paper on which you'll make your drawings. You can make photocopies of the grid paper at the back of this book if you need more drawing paper.

Throughout this book, the sketches start with larger basic shapes. Draw the full shape, even if all of it will not be seen in the final drawing. You can erase the part you don't need later. In each step you will add more detail until you have the finished drawing. The steps are colored to show exactly what to draw when. The drawing for each new step is shown with red lines, while the lines from previous steps are shown in gray.

Each drawing is shown on a grid, and grid pages are provided at the end of the book. The grid is a tool to make copying the drawings easier. While you copy the step-by-step drawings, look closely at how the lines and shapes fit on the grid, and copy them onto your grid sheet. Watch where the lines come close to the grids and where they cross over them. Match them on your grids to copy the steps.

After all the steps are drawn, use a felt-tip pen to go over the pencil lines. Ink over only the lines you need in the final drawing. After giving the felt-tip ink some time to dry so it won't smear, use an eraser to erase the extra pencil lines.

And there's your completed drawing! Now you are ready to add color!

How to Color Your Drawings

Now that the line art is finished, you are ready to color the drawings. Start coloring with things that are familiar to you. If you enjoy coloring with crayons, use them. When you get more comfortable with coloring, you can try other methods such as colored pencils, watercolor paints, markers, or even colored chalk. Try different techniques on the drawings to see what looks best.

When you are ready to start coloring, pick colors that seem to fit the vehicle in the drawing. Be creative! Start by lightly adding the main color to the drawing. Some of the vehicles may already have designs on them, so you can use several different colors if you would like to. Remember to keep the colors light in the beginning—it is much easier to make a color more dark than it is to make it less dark. After the main color is finished, gently add darker colors to areas that would be in shadows or less light. This is usually toward the bottom or underneath the shapes of the vehicles. Adding colors this way is called shading and helps make the drawing look more realistic.

After shading, add lighter colors where more light would be. This is called highlighting, and it is usually done on the top areas of the shapes in the drawing. Just think of sunlight coming down and lighting the vehicle from above.

Look at the color pictures in the book, and try to copy the light and dark shading of the colors. Once you fill in all the colors, your construction vehicle illustration is complete!

Cement Truck

For big jobs that need lots of cement,

this truck carries it right where it is needed!

1 For the cement truck, start by drawing the shapes that make up the front fender, hood, and grille.

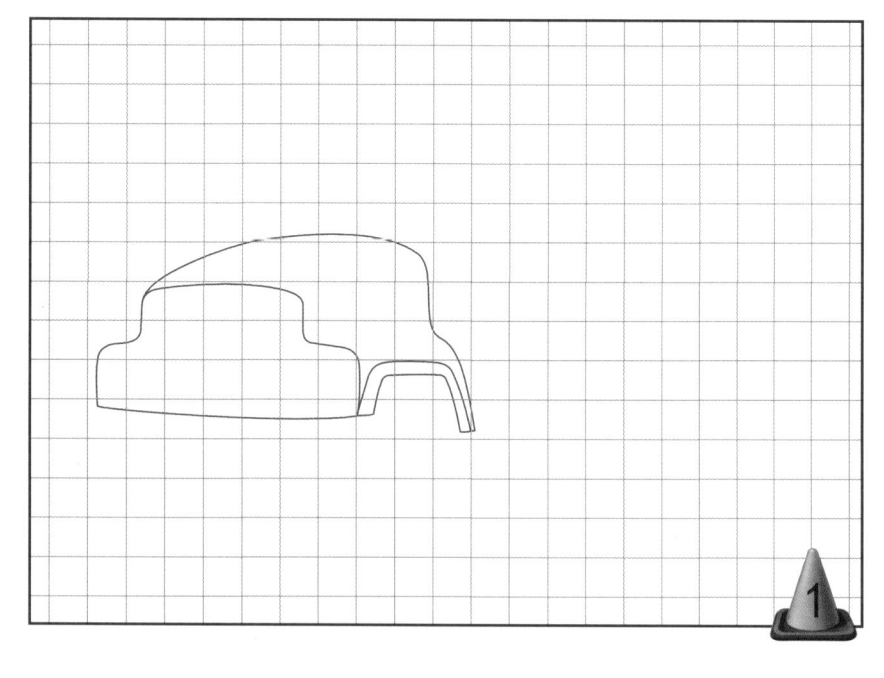

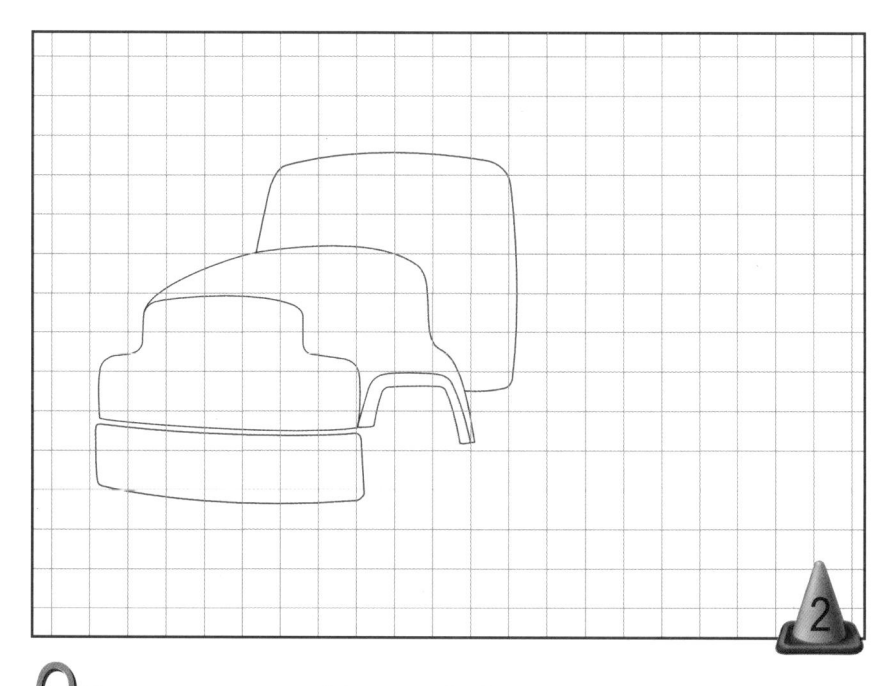

2 Draw a square with rounded corners behind the shape you just drew. This is the cab. Just below the grille, draw a slightly curved rectangle to make the front bumper.

3 Put windows in the cab. The front windshield is a curved rectangle and the side window is a rounded, squarish shape. Draw the front wheel facing you as shown; draw the wheel on the other side of the truck.

4 Draw a square shape below the cab; add a small rectangle at the top of this square. Draw a rounded shape with a circle at the front end for the gas tank. Draw the rear fender, outlining it to add depth.

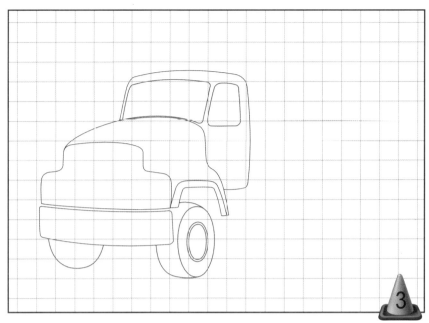

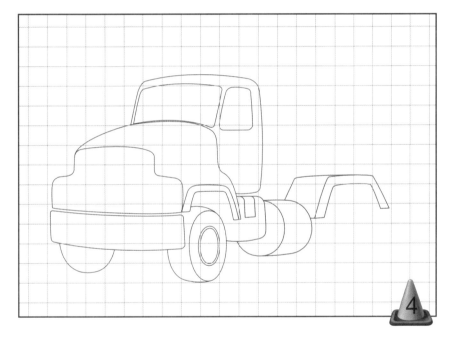

5 Draw the rear tires; there are three tires you can see from this angle. Draw the arm that holds the cement barrel in place; this piece starts behind the gas tank and goes up to behind the cab—it is slightly bent where it touches the cab. Add a very small straight line right behind the door.

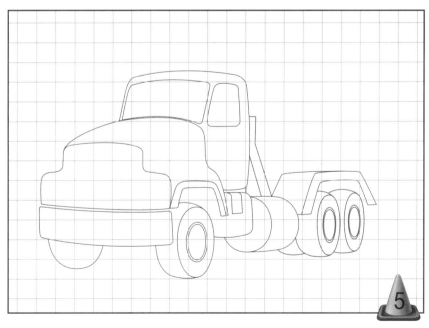

6 Draw the cement barrel. It looks a bit like the body of a bee! It is made up of three overlapping circles with a rounded triangle at the end.

7 Add details such as the two hooks on the front bumper, the wheel hubs, and the rear mud flap (behind the rear wheels). To finish the cement barrel, draw two semi-circles, one in front of the other, at the front of the cement barrel (right behind the cab). Draw the ladder and platform at the back of the cement barrel. There are lots of lines to follow here. Study the picture, and use a ruler to make straight lines.

8 Finish all the details of the cab. Draw rectangular side mirrors, with two narrow rectangles attaching each mirror to the side of the cab. Draw four lights and the top of the exhaust pipe above the windshield. Inside the cab, draw the top of the steering wheel. Draw the side and back windows, adding the line of the cement barrel.

9 Draw and outline two squares for the headlights. Draw a large rectangle with five rectangles inside it—all have rounded corners—on the grille. Add the small line behind the front tire.

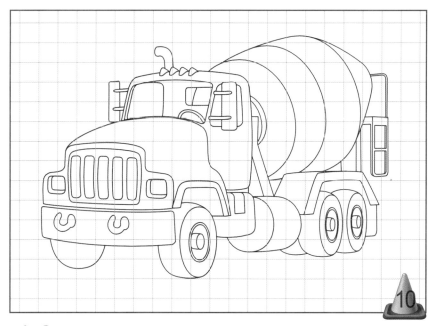

10 Use a felt-tip pen to trace over the lines you want to keep, and erase the extra pencil lines. You can draw a cement truck!

Roller

Rollers flatten roads when they are being paved—
no one wants a bumpy road!

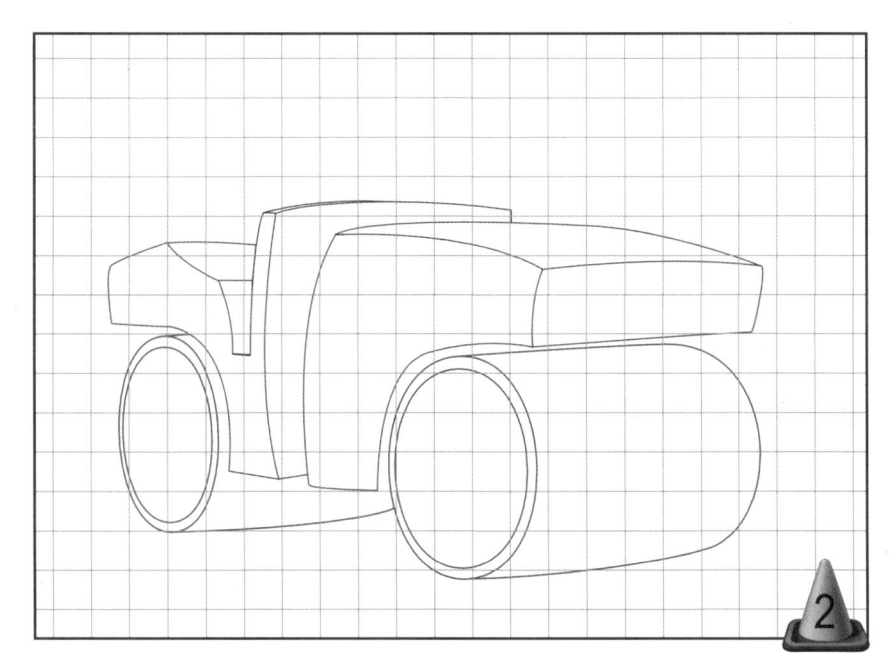

1 Start with the two pieces that make up the body of the roller. Study the drawing, and look at the different shapes—then draw what you see.

2 To make the rollers, draw two large circles. Draw a slightly smaller circle inside each large circle to create a ring. For the front roller, make the ring look like a cylinder by drawing a rectangular shape with a rounded end. Draw the rear roller as shown.

3 Attach the rollers to the vehicle by drawing an axle bracket on top of each roller. Be sure the axle ends nearest the ground are rounded.

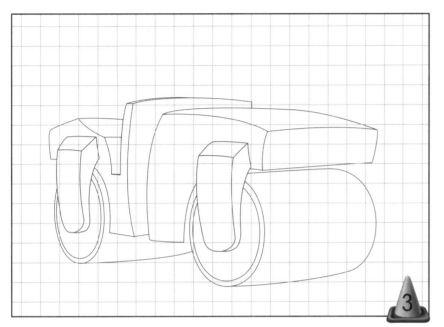

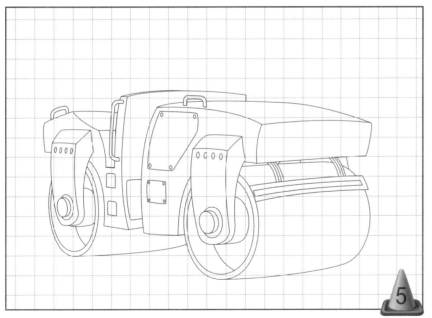

4 Draw the lines inside the rollers that add depth and that create the axles. Add all the circles outside the axle brackets that connect the rollers to the brackets. Draw four small ovals at the top of each axle bracket. Draw the small lines that make the axle brackets on the other side of the body, along with the small line from the bottom of the body to the front roller.

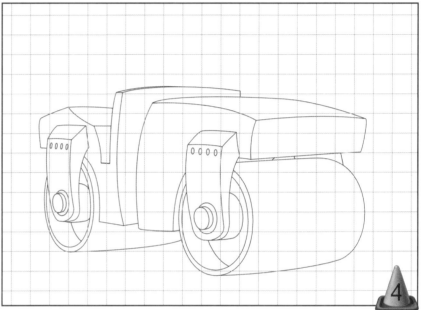

5 Add the handles and railings for the roller operator. Draw square shapes for the side panels. The two front side panels have a circle at each corner—draw those in. Draw a long rectangle on the front roller; make it slightly longer than the roller; this is the scraper bar. Draw a smaller rectangle inside the first. Attach the scraper bar to the body with four lines on either side of the bar.

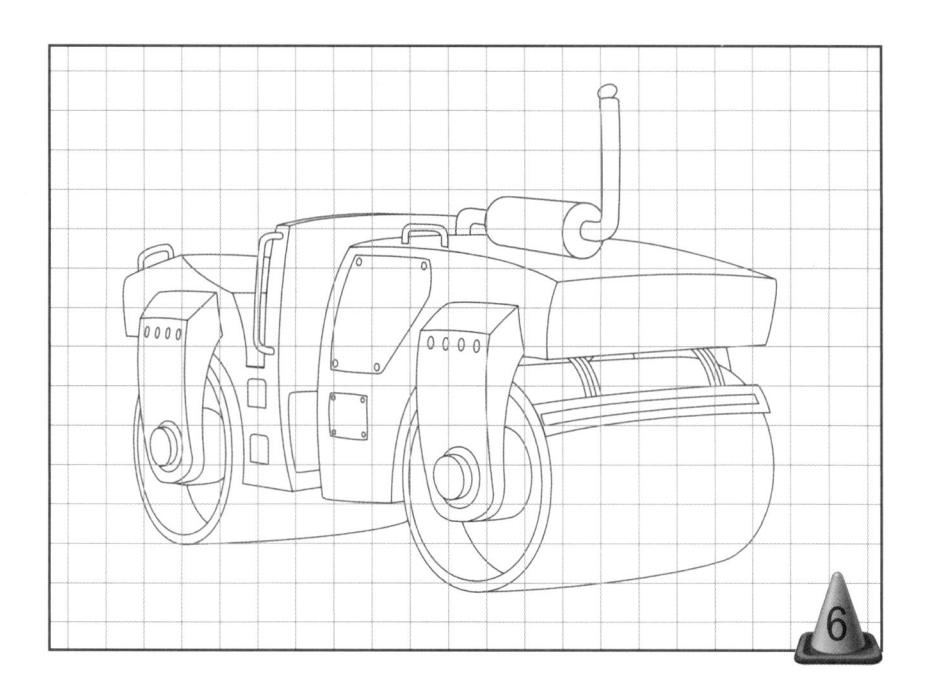

6 Draw the muffler—it is a cylinder with an L-shaped pipe running through it. Draw a circle at the top of the pipe.

7 Draw the seat, being sure to add all the lines and shapes that make it look real. Draw a circle for the steering wheel, adding all the other lines that add depth. Add a safety light on the body in front of the steering wheel. Draw two round headlights on the front of the body; add outlines for depth.

8 Use a ruler to draw the diagonal lines in the rectangle behind the headlights.

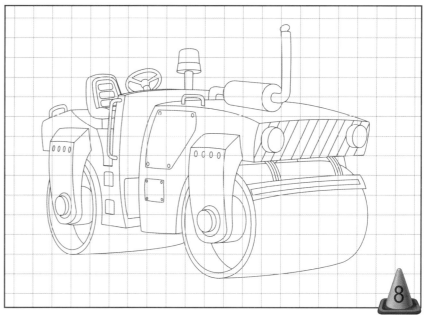

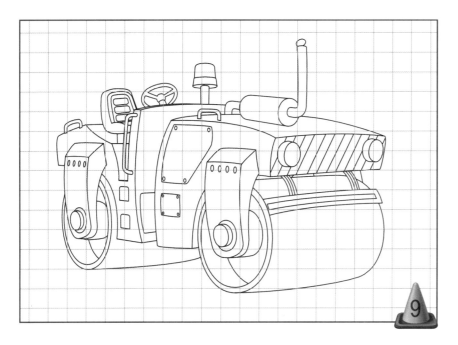

9 Use a felt-tip pen to trace over the lines you want to keep, and erase the extra pencil lines. You can draw a roller!

Excavator

Though it may look like a creature from outer space, this vehicle is useful for digging up dirt!

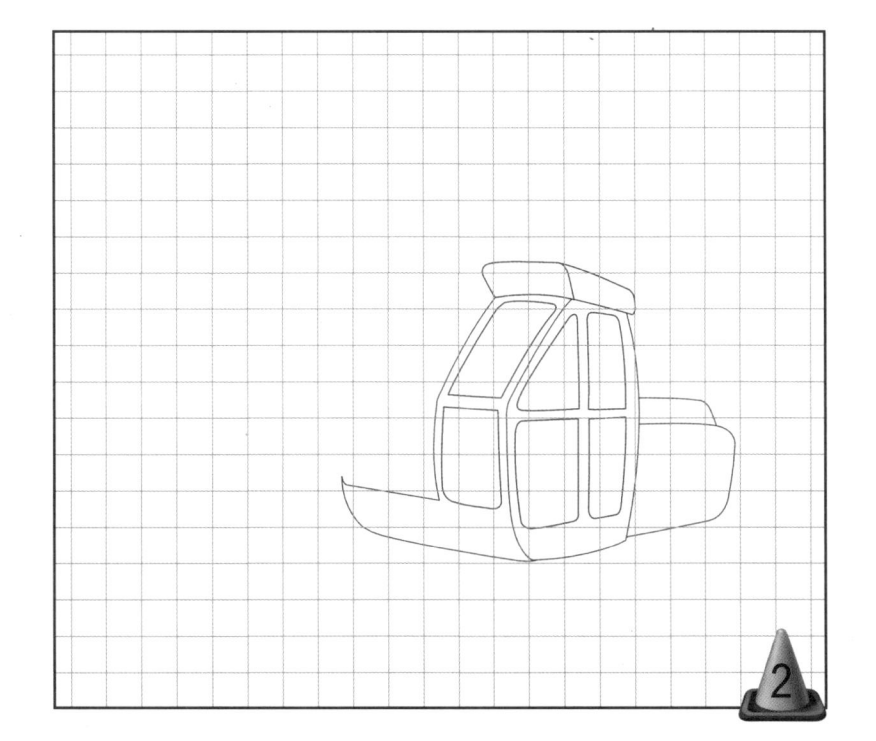

1 Draw the shapes that make up the excavator's cab and platform.

2 Add windows on the cab. There are two in front of the cab and four on the side. Add a roof by drawing two rounded rectangular shapes side by side.

14

3 Draw two circles on the front of the roof and a safety light on top. Draw a muffler, which is a rectangle with a curved pipe running through it. Draw a circle at the top of the pipe.

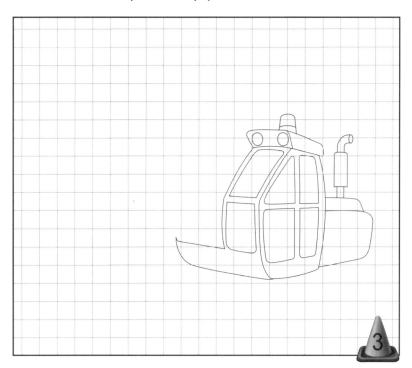

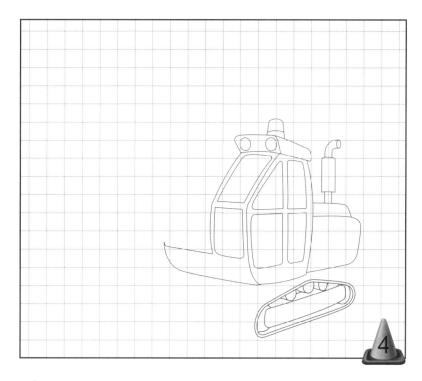

4 To draw the track, start with a rounded triangle and draw another triangle just inside the first one. Inside the triangle, draw a rectangle and add a circle at each end. Draw three more circles above the rectangle, adding additional lines for depth. Look at the example to make sure you place all the shapes correctly.

5 Draw the track on the far side; here only some of the parts can be seen. Finish the tracks by using a ruler to draw evenly spaced lines around the outside of each one for tread.

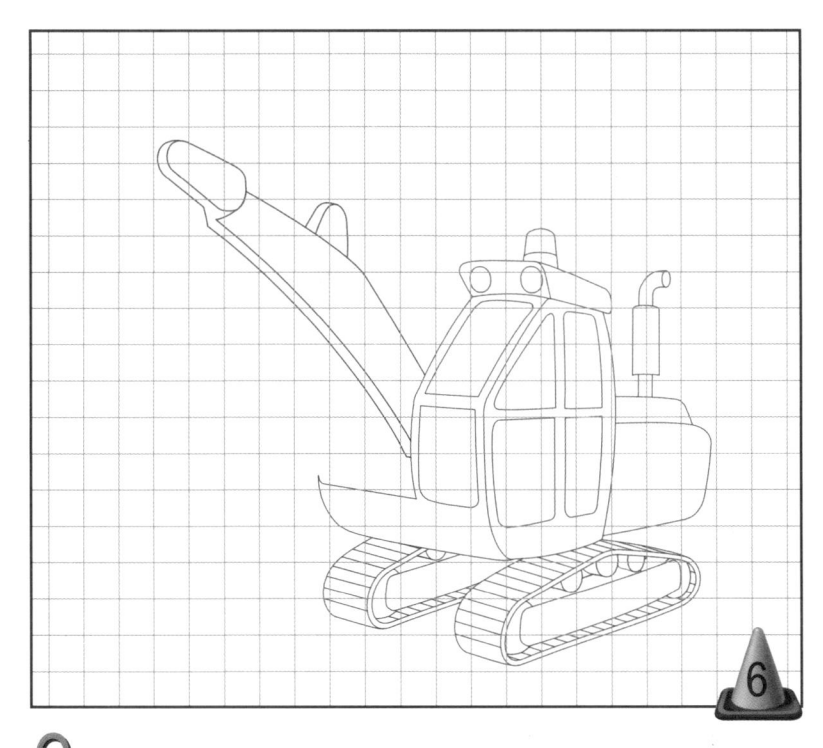

6 Draw the arm of the boom—the top line bends slightly. Just above the bend, draw a rounded triangle; add outline for depth. At the top of the boom, draw a long oval shape. Outline the boom arm to add depth.

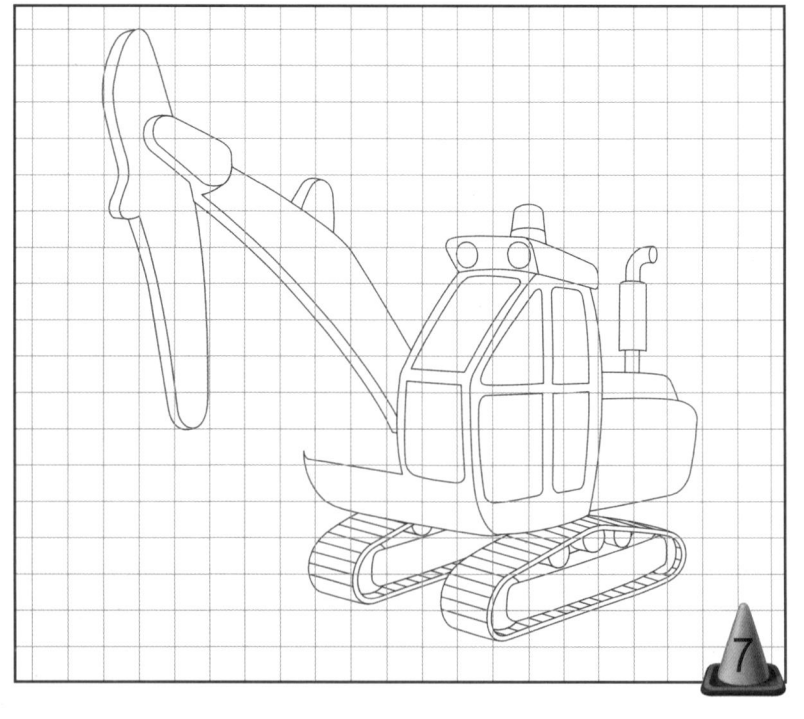

7 Draw the shape that makes up the bottom of the boom. Outline it to add depth.

8 To draw the bucket, make a large half-oval shape. Add the inside rounded line, which echoes the first oval shape. Draw the line from the top to the bottom of the oval, but notice how the line is slightly bent. At the top of the bucket, draw two triangle shapes with rounded tops; outline them to add depth. Add lines to create the triangle behind the bottom of the boom.

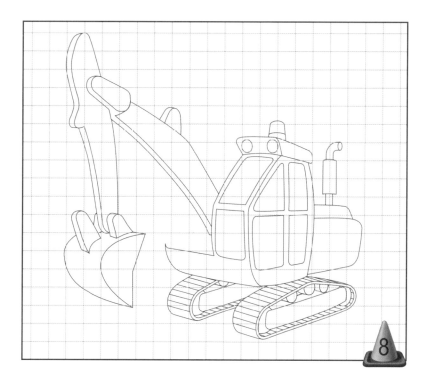

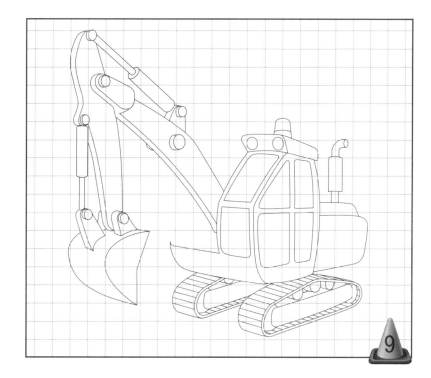

9 Add circles for the pivot joints, which allow the boom and bucket to move up and down. Outline each circle for depth. Draw the two hydraulic cylinders.

10 Draw the two hydraulic cylinders that attach the boom to the body of the cab. Draw the line behind the cylinders to complete the platform.

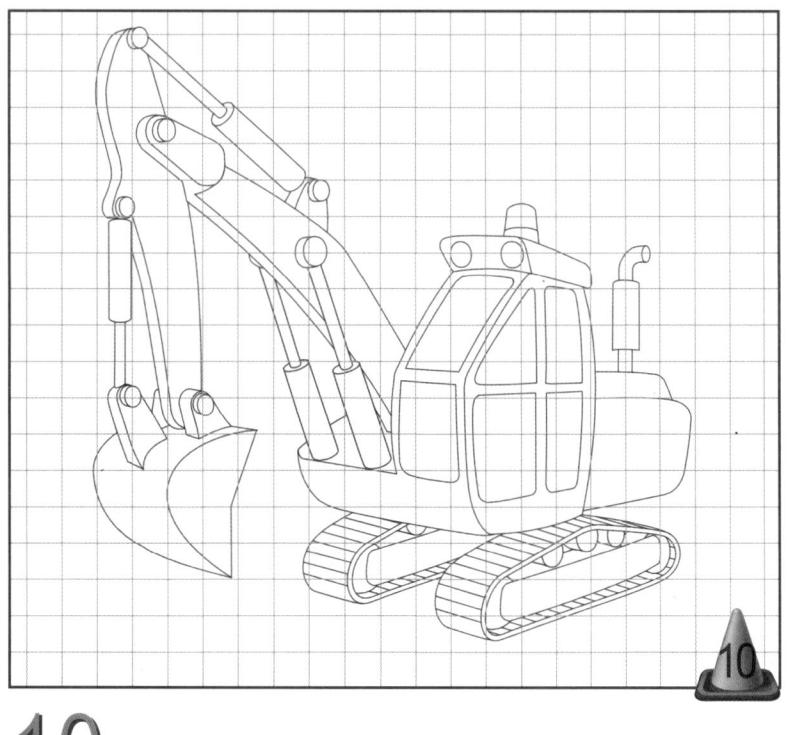

11 Use a felt-tip pen to trace over the lines you want to keep, and erase the extra pencil lines. You can draw an excavator!

Bulldozer

The bulldozer moves earth around—making it a handy vehicle on any construction site!

1 To make the wheels that run the track, draw the five small circles on the bottom; add outlines to add depth. On either side of the five circles, draw two rings. Outline the farthest ring to add depth. Above the circles, draw two more rings; add outlines to add depth.

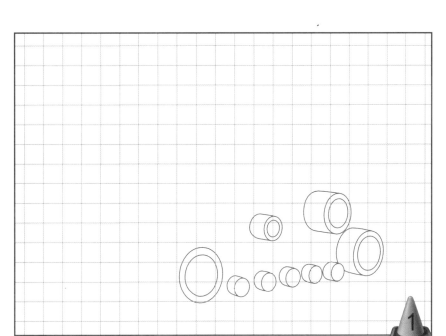

2 Draw a rectangular shape over the bottom wheels; notice how the shape bends down at either end. Draw a similar, smaller shape inside the first. Use a ruler to keep your lines straight. Add outlines to add depth.

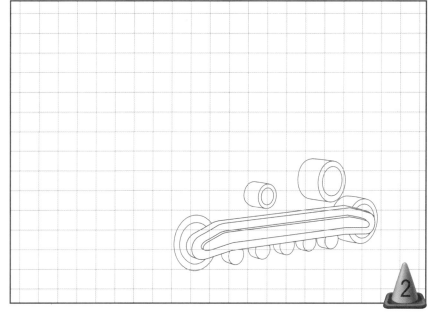

19

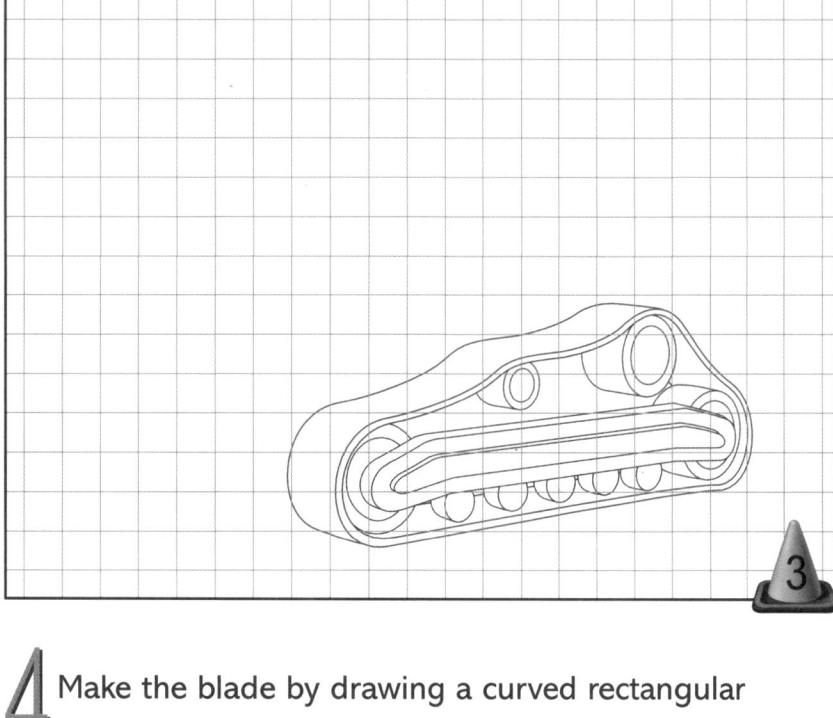

3 Draw a line around all the circles; make another line just outside the first. Draw the outside line to make the side edge and face of the track. Also notice the small lines you need to make on the inside of the track.

4 Make the blade by drawing a curved rectangular shape; add the tab to the top middle of the rectangle. Draw the sides of the blade and the details as shown.

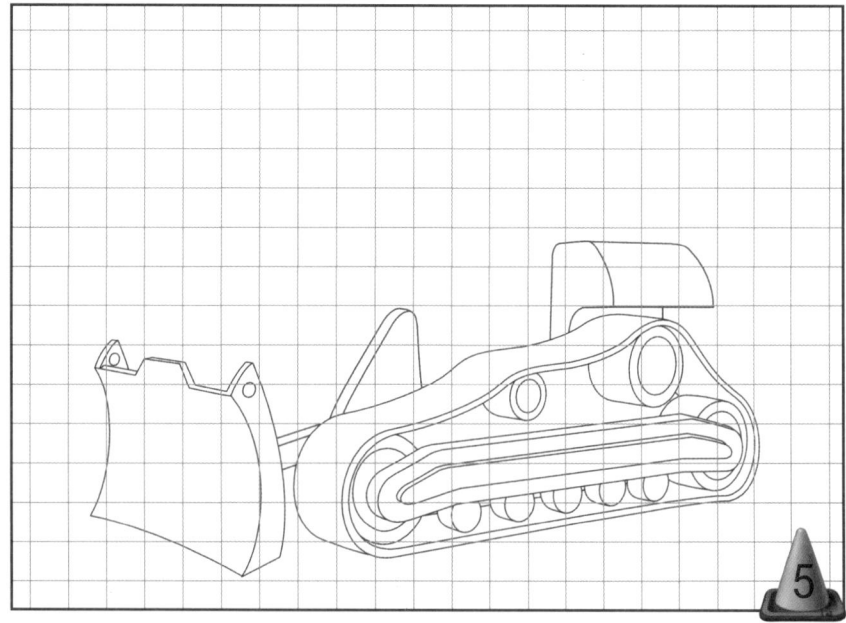

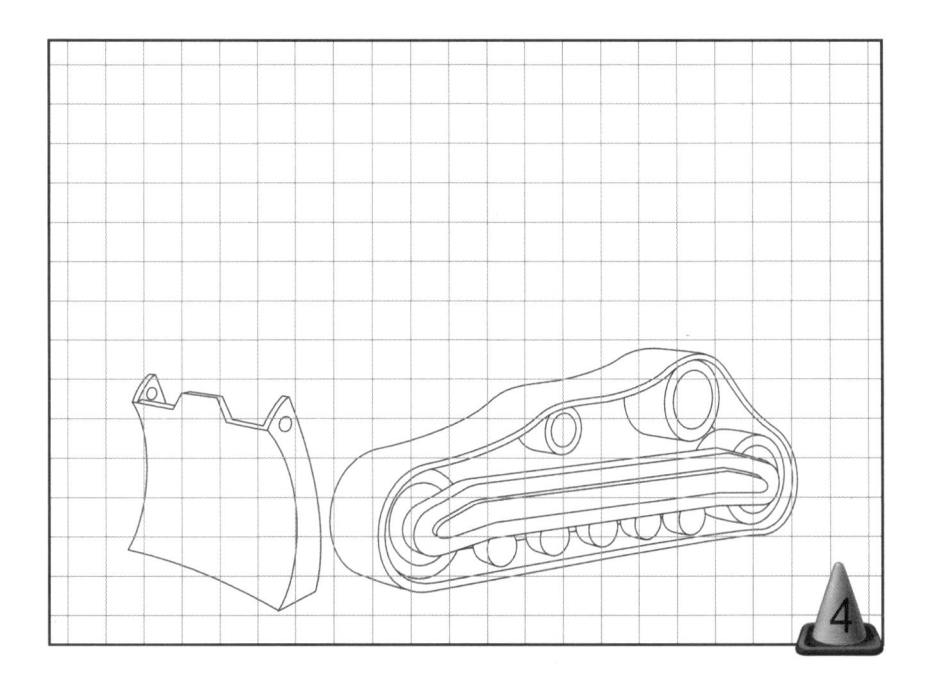

5 Draw the rounded triangle and rectangle that make up the lift arm that connects the blade to the bulldozer; add outlines for depth. Draw the fender—follow the example shown.

6 For the hood, make a square shape with a tab at the fender. Draw outlines where shown. On the front of the hood, draw the grille, which is a rectangle with the top edges rounded.

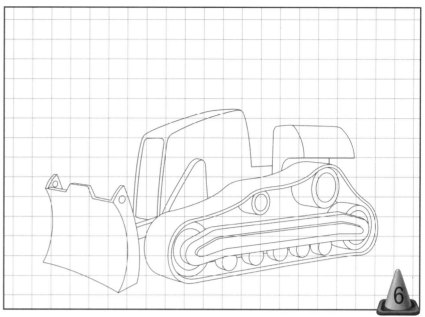

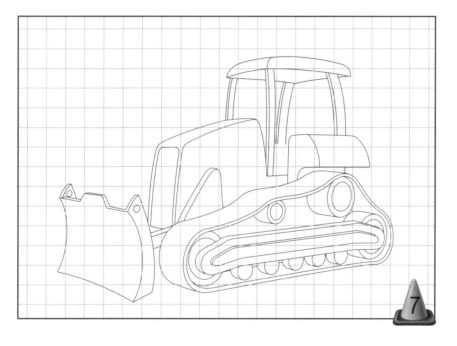

7 To make the cab, draw four thin, slightly curved rectangles. Outline each rectangle for depth. Draw the roof as shown.

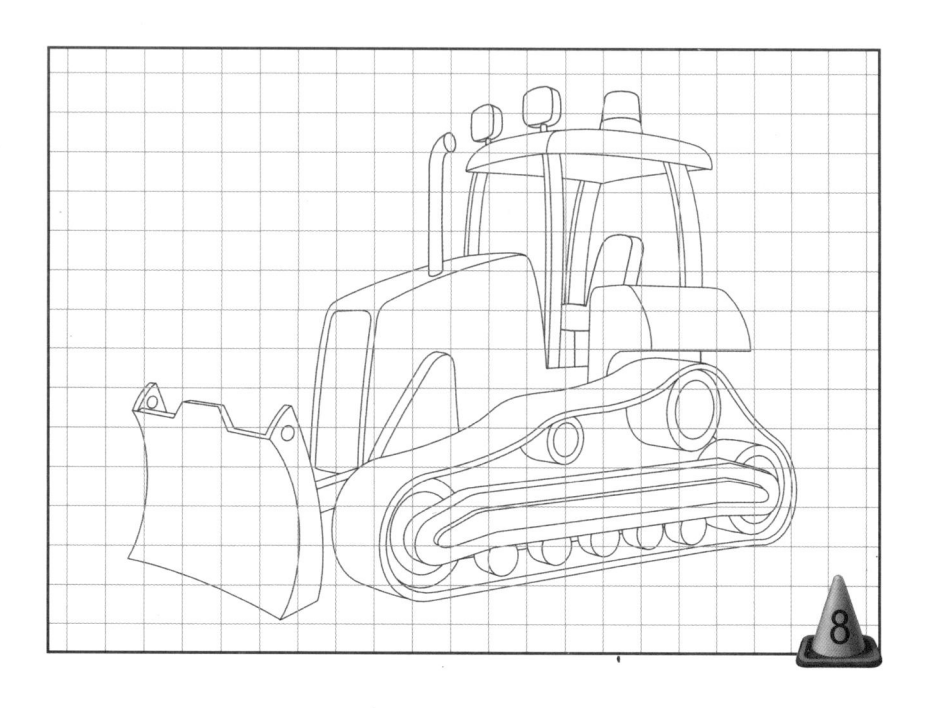

8 Draw the driver's seat in the cab, and add two headlights and a safety light on top of the roof. On the hood, draw a curved exhaust pipe. Add a circle to the top of the pipe.

9 Draw the three vents in the hood; each vent is a little larger than the one above it. Draw a hydraulic cylinder from the triangular part of the lift arm to below the fender. Look carefully, and draw the other lines that finish the body of the dozer.

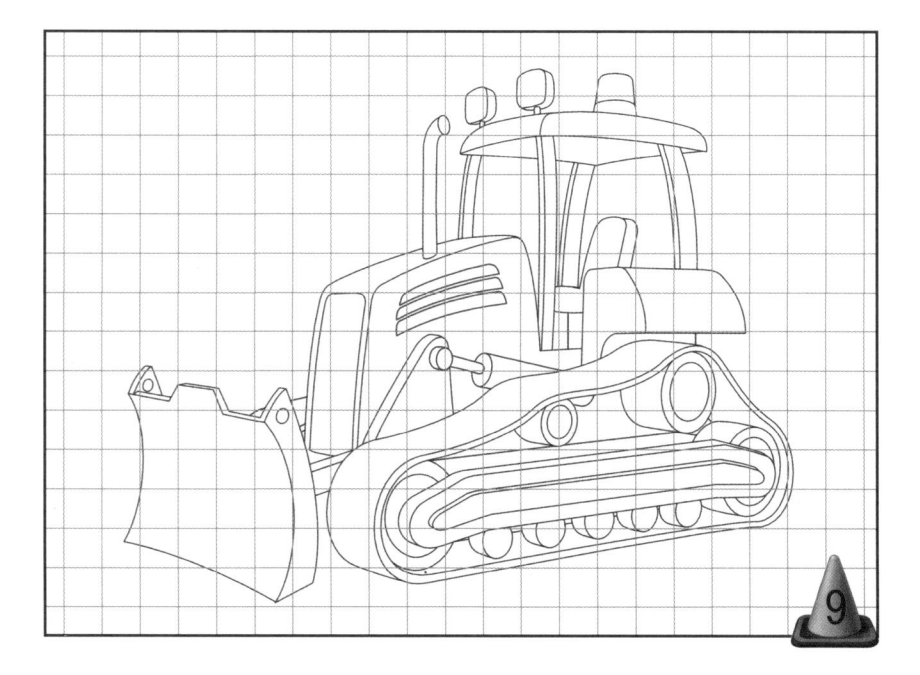

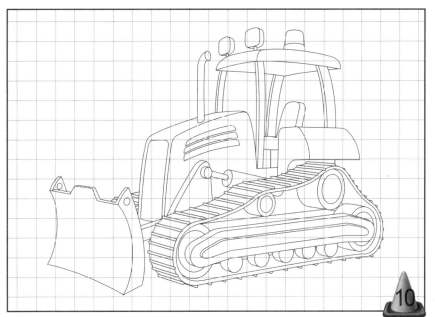

10 Draw cleats on the tread faces. Use a ruler to make the many small, evenly spaced rectangles on top of the track. On the back and underside of the tread, the cleats look like small, triangular bumps.

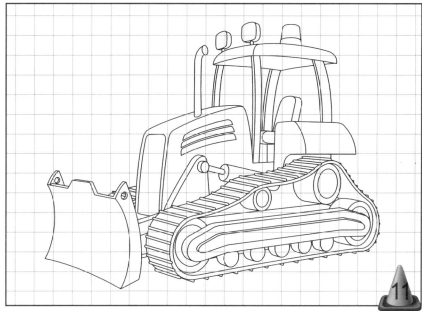

11 Use a felt-tip pen to trace over the lines you want to keep, and erase the extra pencil lines. You can draw a bulldozer!

Crane

This handy vehicle, which needs supports to keep it from tipping over, can reach really high to help move things from place to place.

1 Draw the side of the crane. It is a long shape with rounded cutouts where the wheels will go and a peak near the front for the cab.

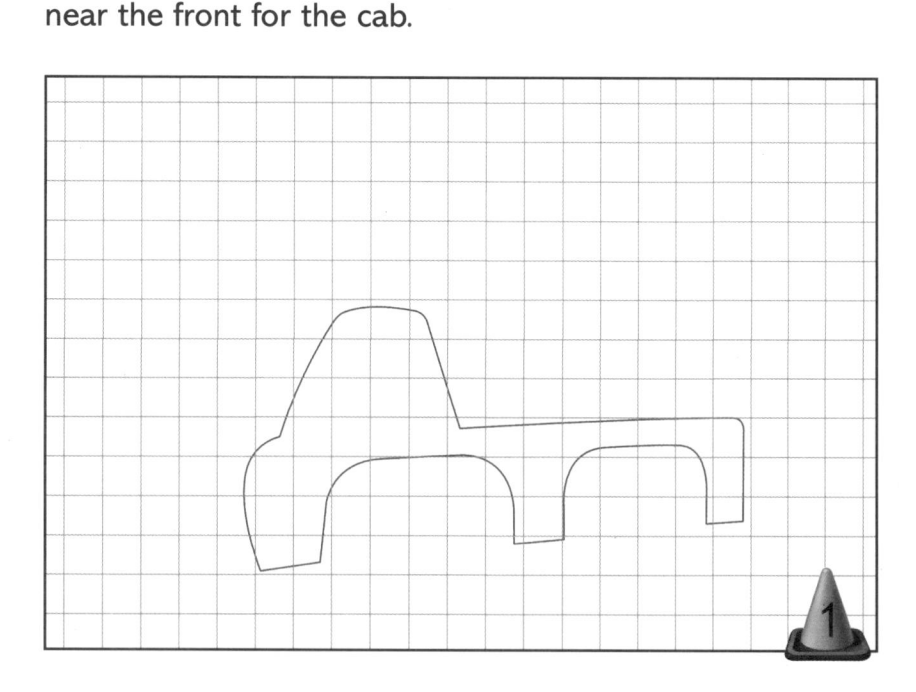

2 Draw four circles inside the cutouts for the wheels. Within these circles draw two circles, one inside the other, so they look like rings.

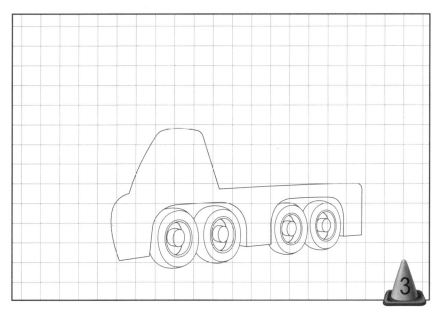

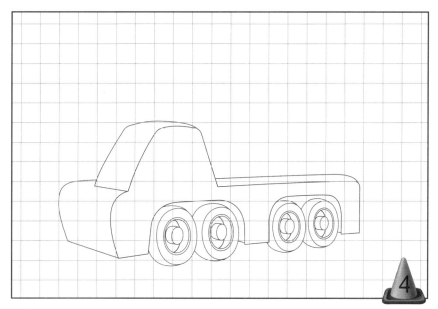

3 Make the tires look real by adding width to the outside. Finish the wheels by drawing the hubs. Also draw the line in each tire that adds depth to the inside of the wheel. Draw a short, horizontal line on the side of the crane body behind each second tire.

4 To build the body of the crane, draw the lines shown. Be sure to make the lines curved or straight where shown. A ruler will be a help here.

5 Draw a rectangular shape for the front windshield and two odd shapes for the side windows. Then draw and outline two squares for headlights on the front of the cab. The front bumper is a long, curved rectangle. Use a ruler to draw evenly spaced diagonal lines on the bumper. Near the back of the truck draw a triangle with a rounded top. Draw a matching line to add depth.

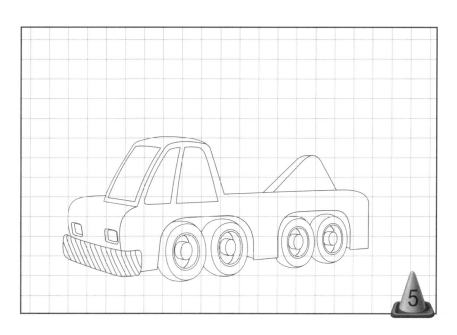

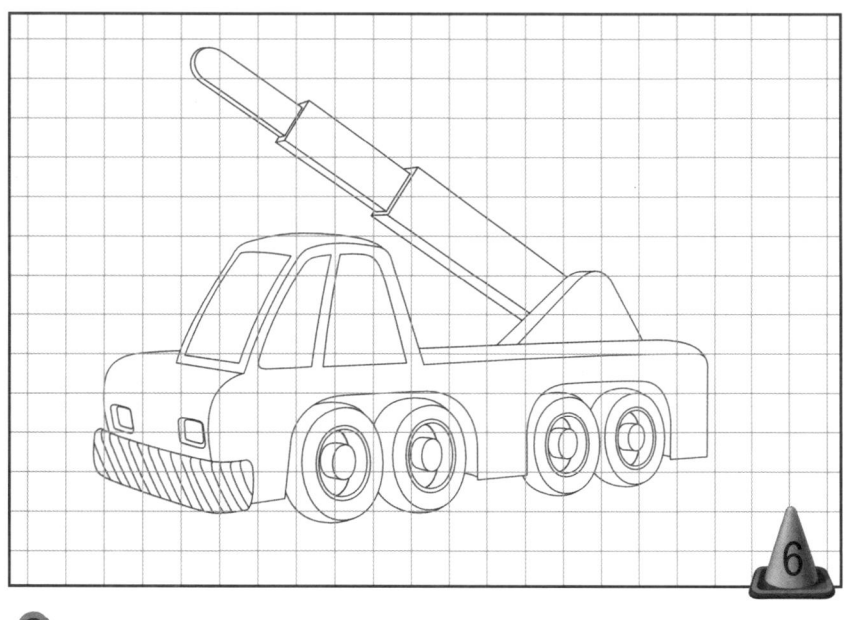

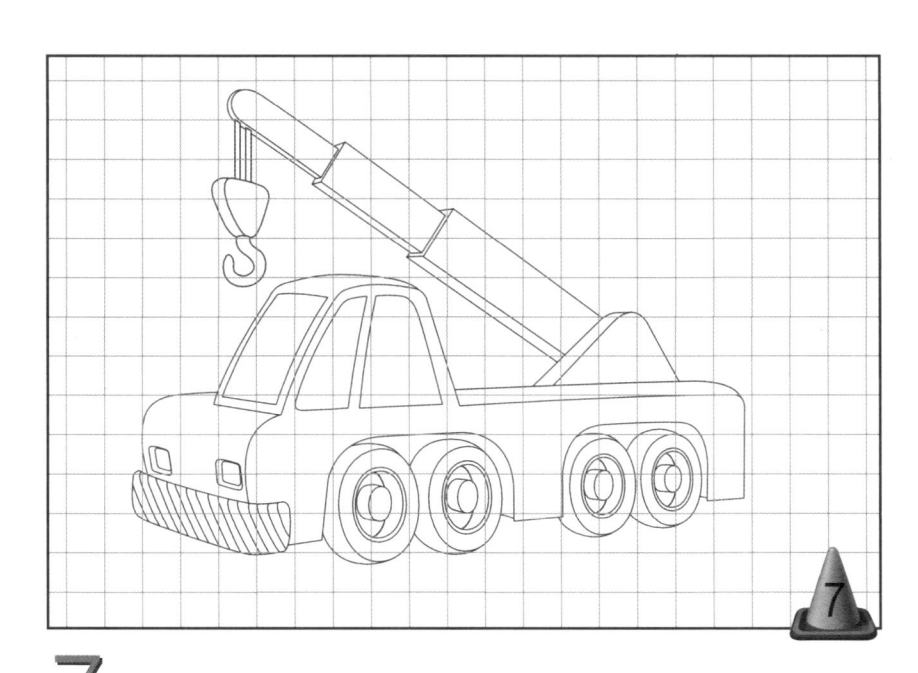

6 Draw the crane arm, which is called the boom. It is made up of three rectangular shapes. Each rectangle is a little shorter and smaller than the previous one. Use your ruler to get the lines straight. Round the end of the top rectangle. Draw the lines that add depth.

7 Draw four lines from the top of the rounded end of the boom. Draw an upside-down triangle at the bottom of the lines. Add the line to the side of the triangle for depth. Draw the hook below the triangle.

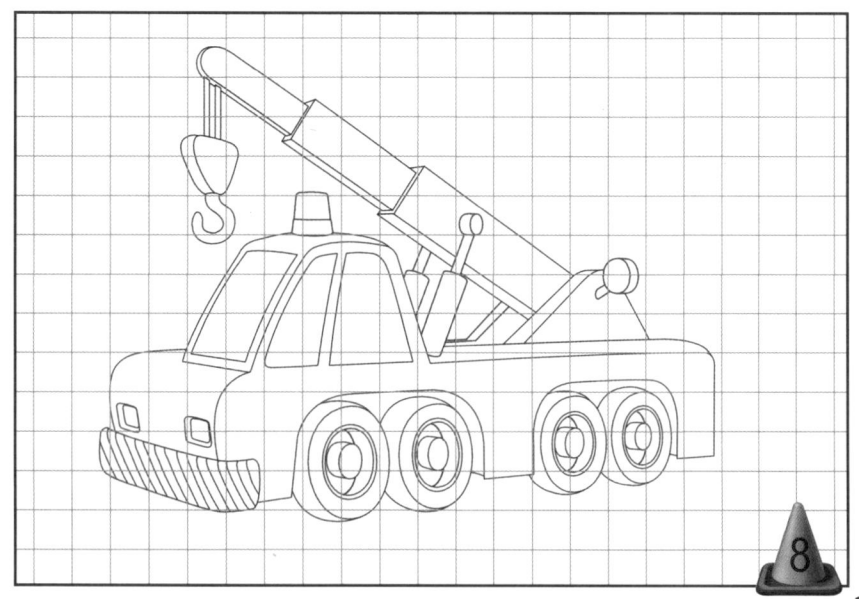

8 To finish the boom, draw the two hydraulic cylinders that raise and lower it. Draw the circle that connects the front cylinder to the boom, adding the circular line to add depth. Draw the taillight. Draw the back triangular arm support, matching the triangular shape you drew in step 5. Add the safety light on the cab's roof.

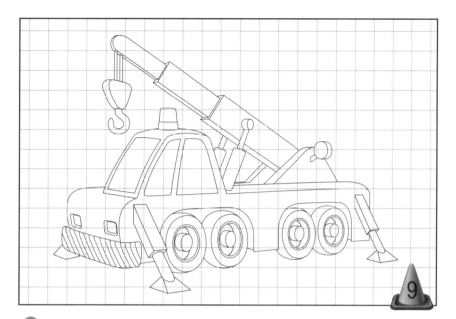

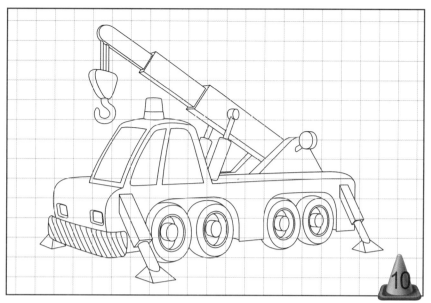

9 Draw the special supports a crane needs to keep it from falling over when it lifts heavy objects. The supports are rectangular shapes, with pyramid shapes at the ends, near the ground.

10 Use a felt-tip pen to trace over the lines you want to keep, and erase the extra pencil lines. You can draw a crane!

Front Loader

A front loader can scoop up dirt and other things that need to be moved and taken out of the way.

1 To make the bucket, draw a rectangle. Draw another one just outside the first. At each end of the rectangles, draw a rounded triangular shape. At the left edge, draw the line to make the rim at the top of the bucket. To make the arm, make a large curved H shape with a bar at top. Draw outlines for depth.

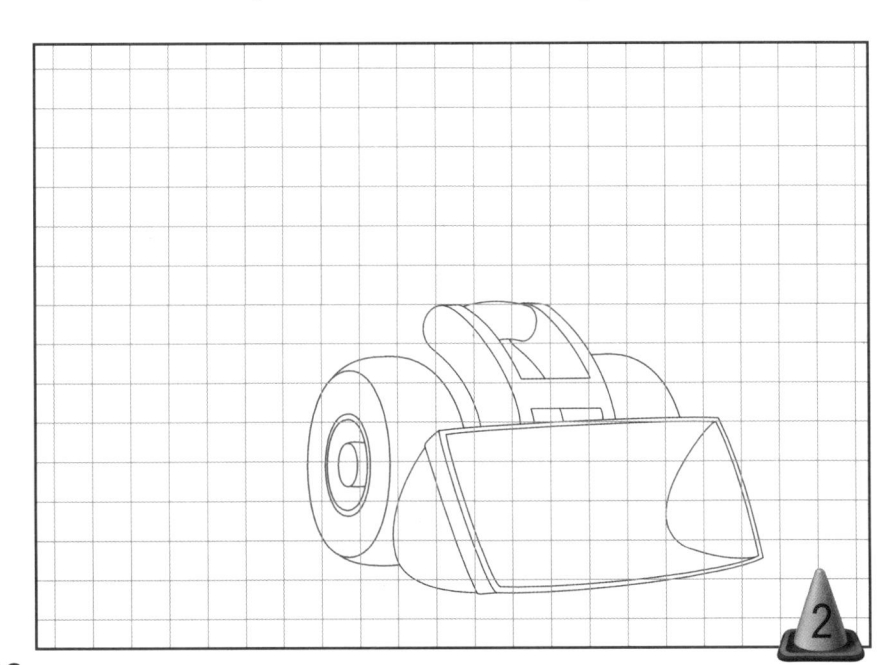

2 Draw the two front wheels. The far wheel is just a curved line. The front wheel includes the tire and hub.

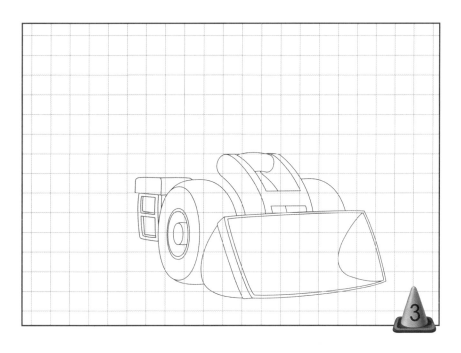

3 Draw the ladder and step the operator uses to get into the cab. The ladder is made up of square and rectangular shapes. Use a ruler to make all the lines straight.

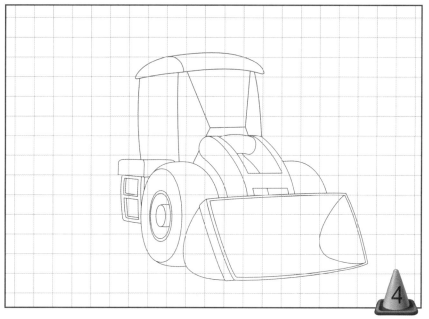

4 To make the cab, draw the two large rectangles for the side and front of the cab. In the front square, add lines that will create a three-dimensional look to the cab. Add the roof as shown.

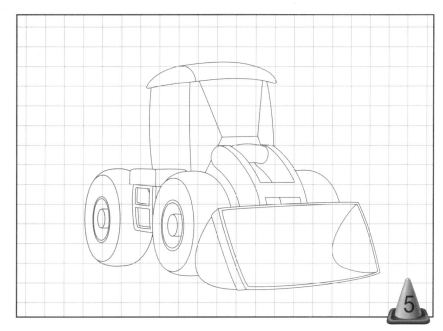

5 Draw the back wheel, which looks like the front wheel. (Be sure to add the tire line you can see through the ladder.)

6 Add tread to the tires as shown. Construction vehicles need large tires with deep grooves so they can drive through mud and dirt. The tread is made up of evenly spaced diagonal lines, which come together at a rounded end on the outside of the tire. (Be sure to add the tread you can see through the ladder.)

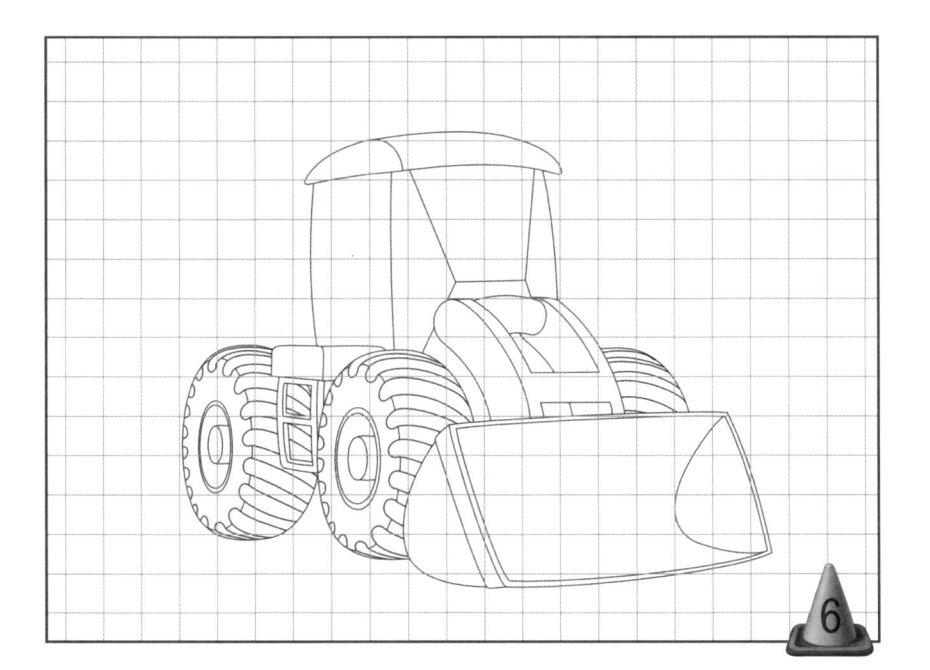

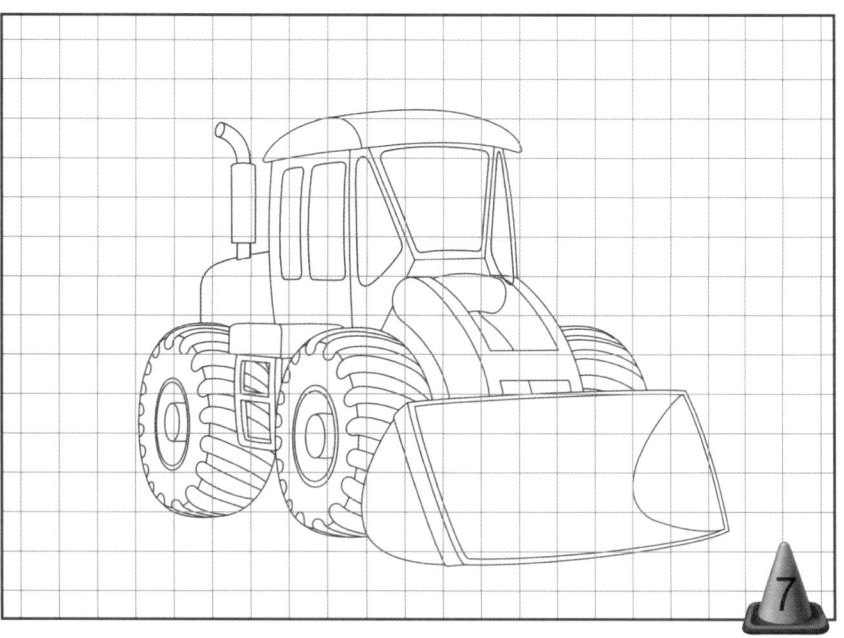

7 Draw five windows in the cab. Notice how each window has a different shape—follow the example. Draw a rounded corner behind the cab for the hood. On top of the hood draw the muffler, which is a rectangle with a pipe running through it. Add a circle at the top of the pipe.

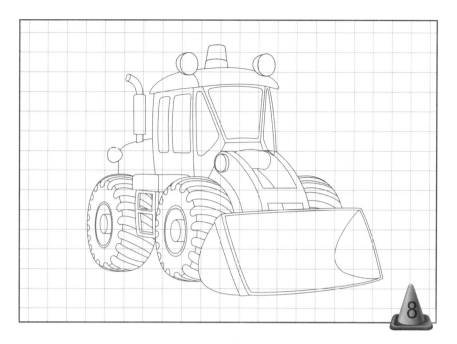

8 Draw the back of the taillight on the hood. On the roof, draw a safety light and two headlights. Add outlines to headlights for depth. Draw a circle on the arm; add outline for depth.

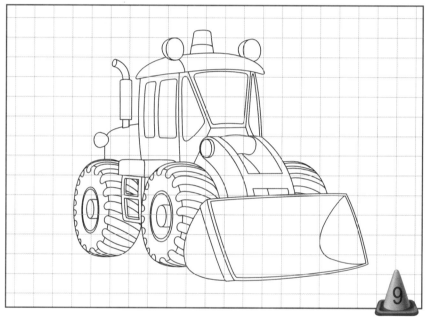

9 Use a felt-tip pen to trace over the lines you want to keep, and erase the extra pencil lines. You can draw a front loader!

Grapple Skidder

A grapple skidder is used by lumberjacks to move big tree trunks around.

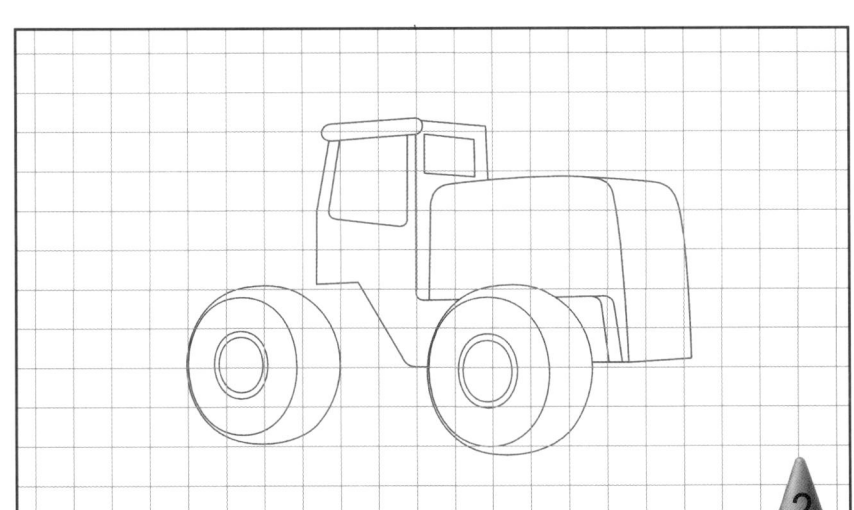

1 Draw a large outside circle for the side wheels. Inside each circle draw three more circles. The two innermost circles are close together.

2 Draw the shapes that make up the cab and the hood of the machine. Look closely, and draw what you see.

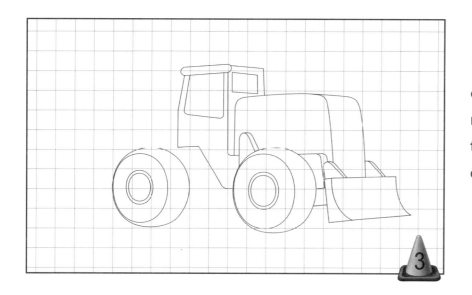

3 To make the blade, draw a curved rectangle for the front of the blade. Draw lines to square off the left edge of the blade. Connect the blade to the machine by making two straight lines back to the front tire. Draw the three rounded triangular shapes; add outlines to create depth.

4 Draw and outline the three pieces that make up the grapple skidder's boom. Be sure to add rounded ends and include the bumps shown. Also draw the platform below the cab.

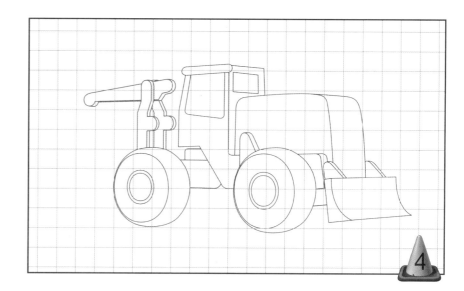

5 To draw the grapple, make a rounded triangular shape; outline the shape to create depth. Draw two short lines to connect the boom to the triangular shape. From the bottom of the triangle, draw and outline the claws. Draw the two hydraulic cylinders that move the boom up and down.

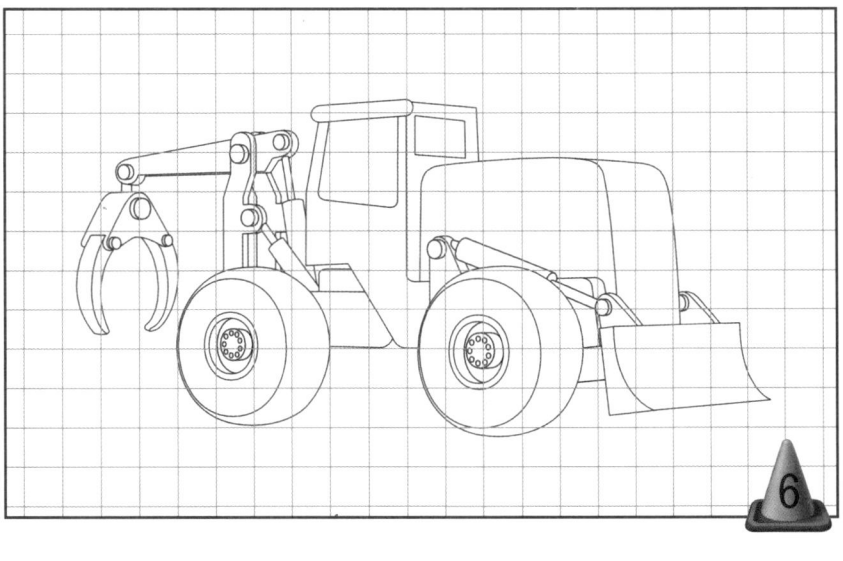

6 Finish the wheels by drawing the hubs. Add the curved lines inside the rings that add depth. Draw all the circles for the pivot points that lift the boom and blade. Outline each circle to add depth. Draw the hydraulic cylinder connected to the blade.

7 To make the grille, draw a rectangle with rounded corners at the front of the hood. Use a ruler to draw eight horizontal lines inside the grille. Draw a triangular shape with rounded corners on the side of the hood. Add the two curved bars that run from the top of the hood to the cab.

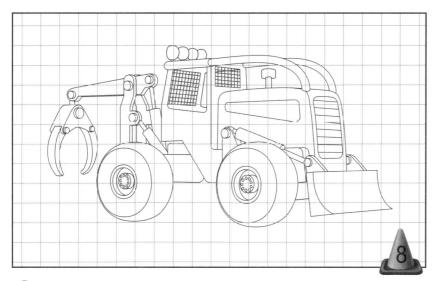

8 Add four round lights to the top of the cab. Draw the exhaust pipe on top of the hood. Draw mesh in the front and back window areas; use a ruler to draw the lines. Add the L-shape line to create the window on the far side of the cab.

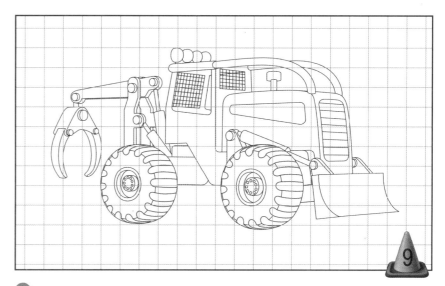

9 Use a ruler to help you draw tread on the tires. The tread is made up of evenly spaced diagonal lines. These lines come together at a rounded end on the outside of the tires.

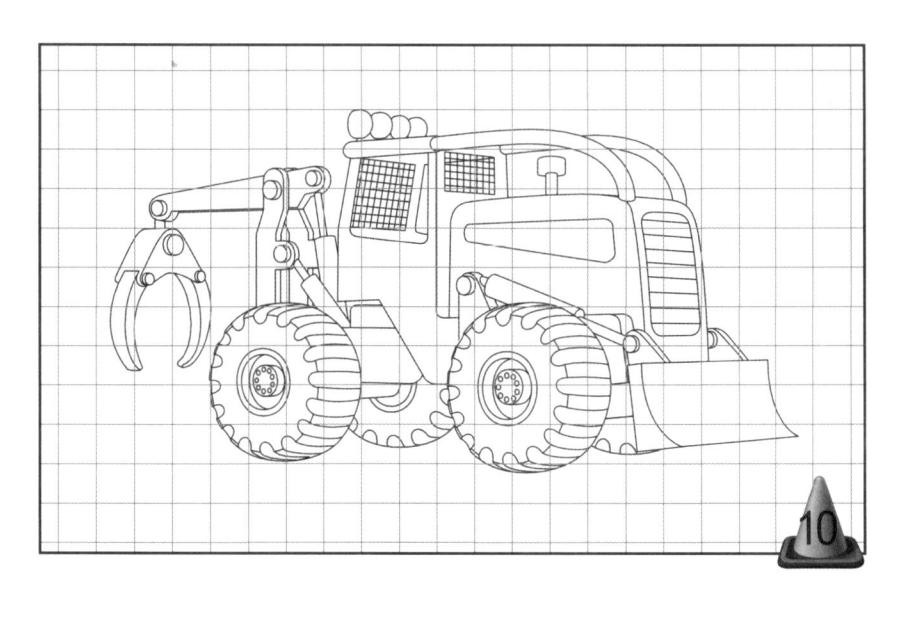

10 Draw the two wheels on the far side of the skidder, including the tread. Add the line for the axle between the back tires.

11 Use a felt-tip pen to trace over the lines you want to keep, and erase the extra pencil lines. You can draw a grapple skidder!

Crawler Drill

The crawler drill is used to make holes in concrete surfaces; it has a very powerful drill!

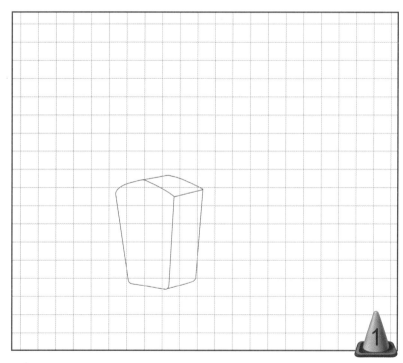

1 Draw the shape that makes up the cab; add outlines for depth.

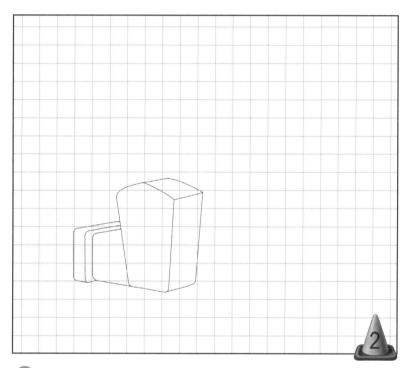

2 Draw the hood, which is a square. Add the upside down L-shape lines outside the square.

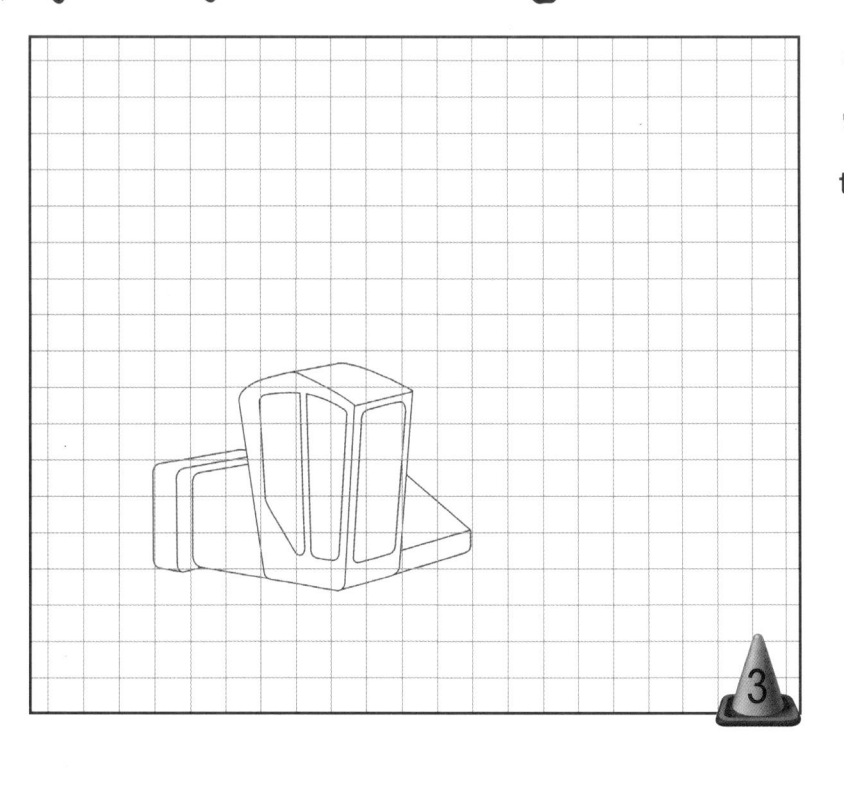

3 Add three windows in the cab. On the far side of the cab, draw a triangle. Add the line to create a three-dimensional look.

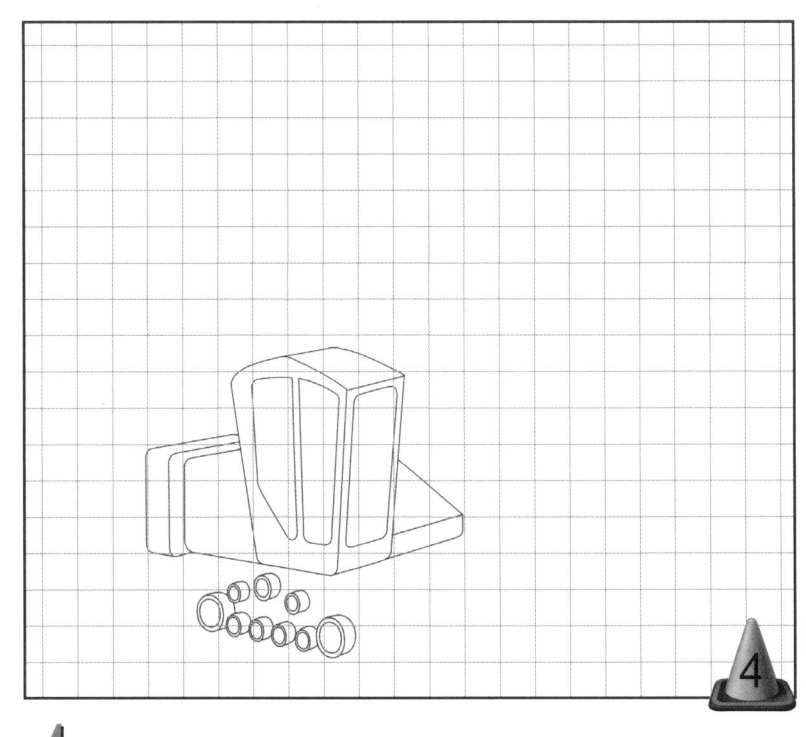

4 To make the tracks, begin by drawing the circles and rings that make up the wheels that run the track. Add outlines for depth.

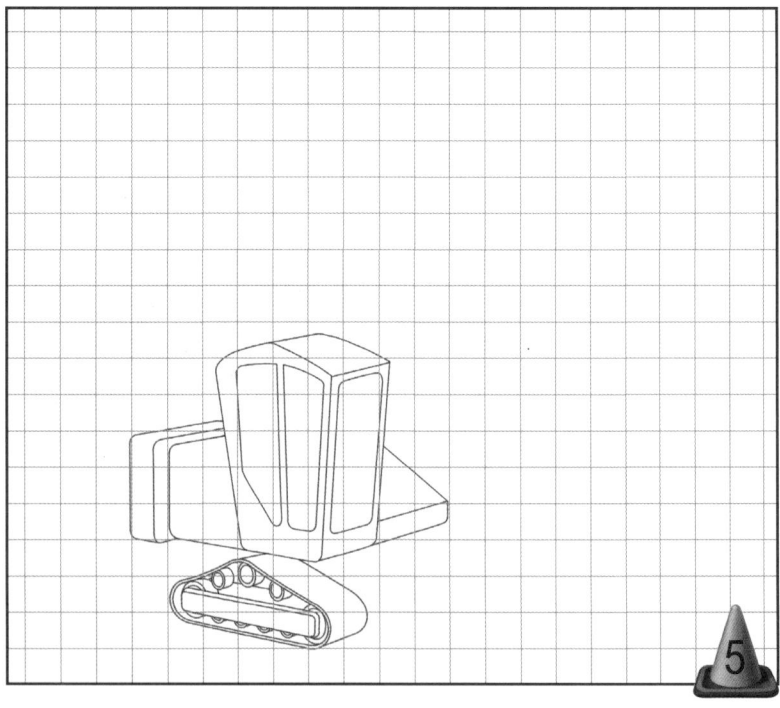

5 Draw a rectangle with rounded corners along the bottom circles; add outline for depth. Draw a rounded triangle around all the circles. Draw another line just outside the first. Add the outside lines to create the face of the track.

6 Draw the part of the far track you can see from this side of the drill. Add the rectangle and lines at the bottom of the cab. Draw the muffler, which is a rectangle with a pipe running through it.

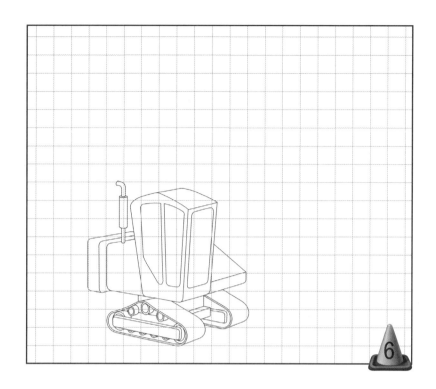

7 Add the circles to the rear track. Use a ruler to draw the tread details on both tracks. Draw and outline the shapes that make up each piece of the boom.

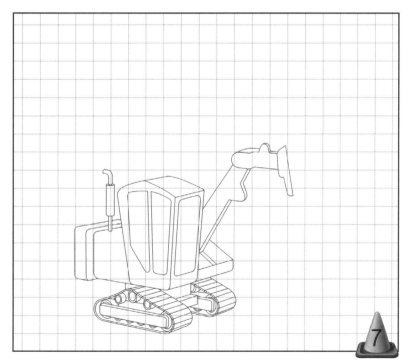

8 To draw the drill, make two almost vertical rectangles side by side, one of which is much longer than the other. Draw the two horizontal rectangles that appear to hold the two long shapes together; add outlines for depth. At the top of the longer rectangle, add the rounded triangle and collar. At the other end, draw a rounded collar and the drill bit, which has a pointed end. Draw and outline the rounded triangular shape at the base of the boom.

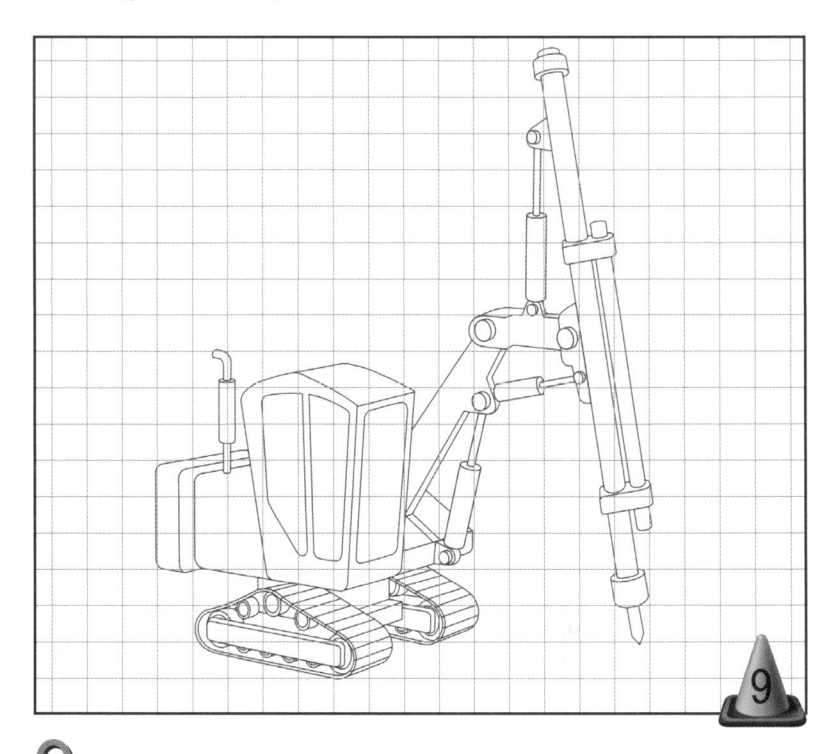

9 Add all the circles for the pivot joints that let the drill move up and down; outline each circle to add depth. Draw the three hydraulic cylinders.

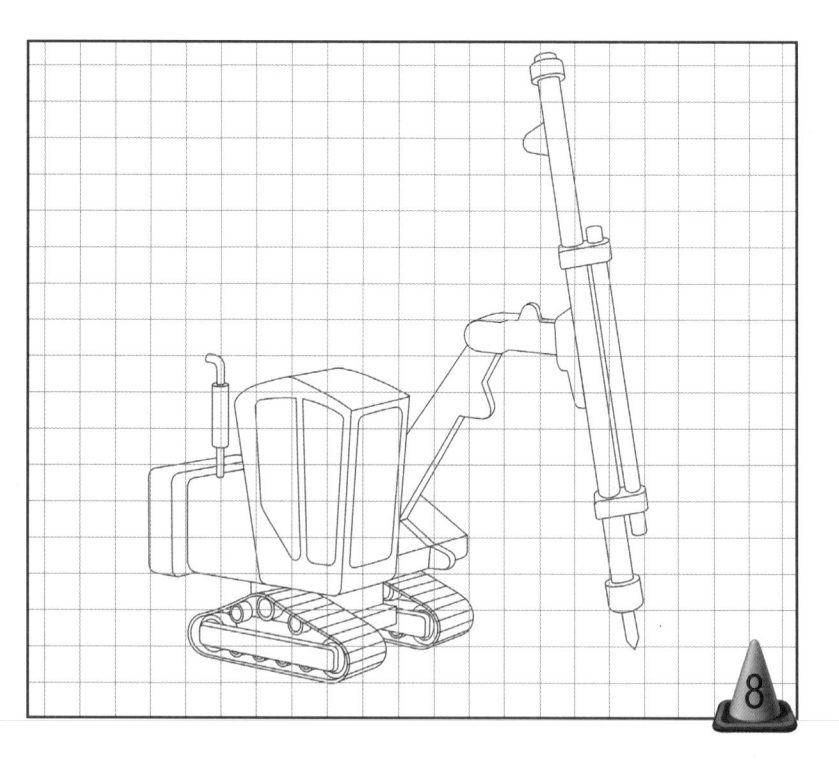

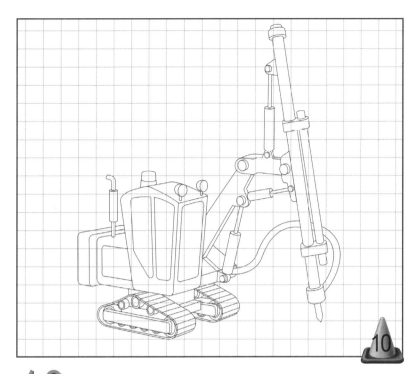

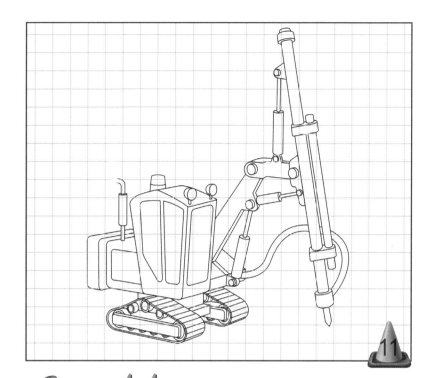

10 Add the two top headlights and the safety light to the top of the cab. Draw the water hose that keeps the drill bit cool. Draw a square on the side of the hood.

11 Use a felt-tip pen to trace over the lines you want to keep, and erase the extra pencil lines. You can draw a crawler drill!

Dump Truck

A dump truck is very useful—
it is used to carry many different things at a construction site.

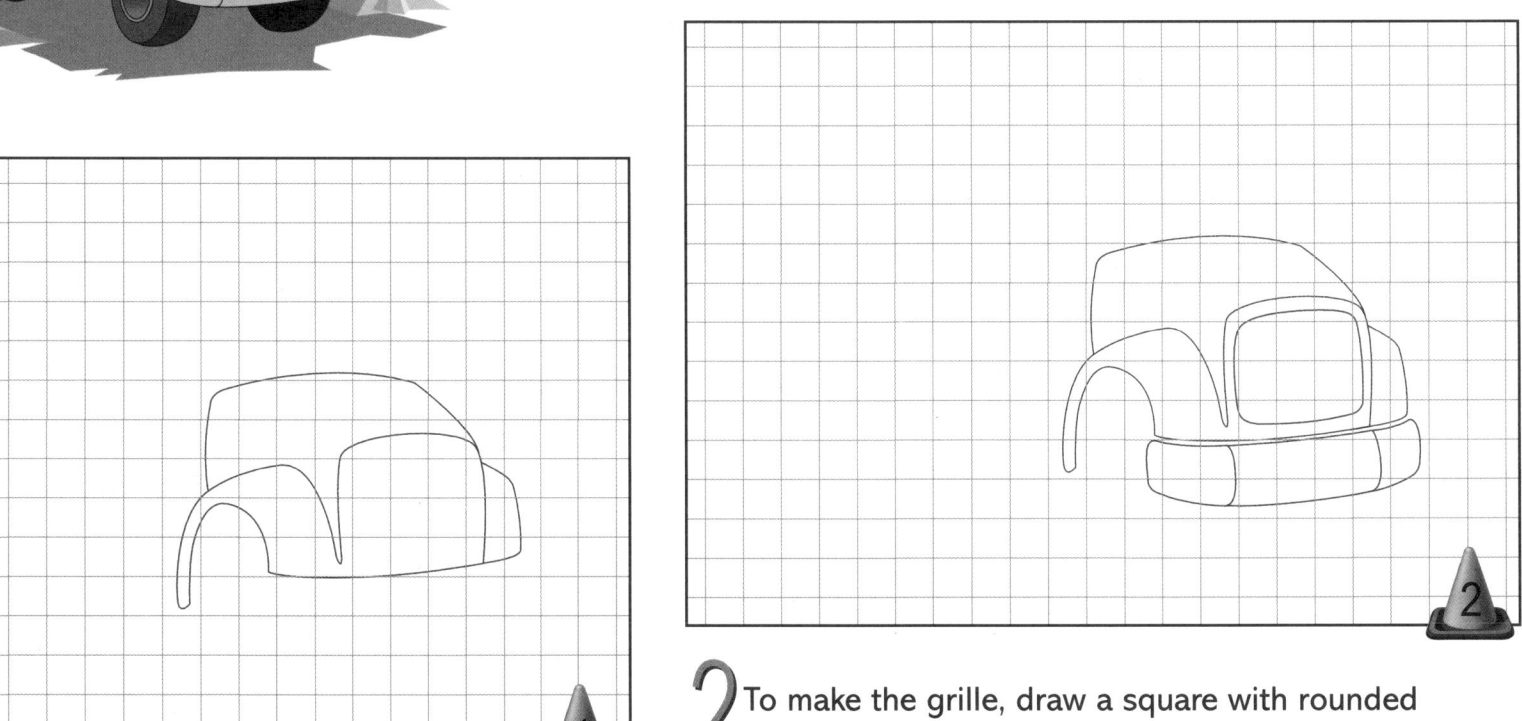

1 Begin at the front of the truck by drawing the shapes that will become the front fenders and hood.

2 To make the grille, draw a square with rounded corners at the front of the hood. Draw a rectangular shape for the front bumper, adding the two slightly curved vertical lines. Be sure the ends of the bumper are slightly narrower than the middle so it looks curved.

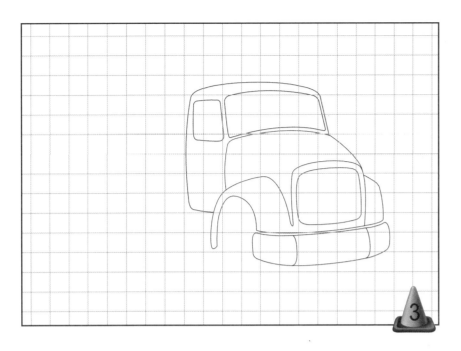

3 Draw the cab—which is squarish with rounded corners. Add a large rectangular shape for the front windshield and a square with rounded corners for the side window.

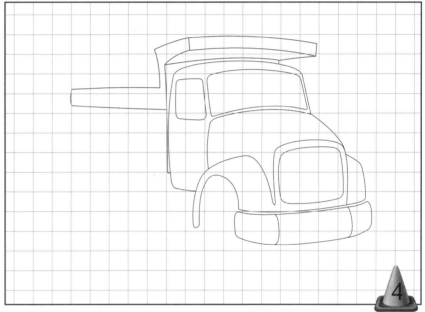

4 A ruler will be helpful for this step since there are many long, straight lines. Draw a sideways L shape as the top of the long bed. Above the cab, draw a rectangle that is about the same width as the cab. Draw in the other lines to connect the L and the rectangle.

5 Draw a rectangular shape from the cab to the back end of the L. This is the side of the truck. Inside this rectangle, draw slightly curved rectangles with triangles inside them to give the side of the dump truck a pattern. Look carefully at each shape, and draw what you see.

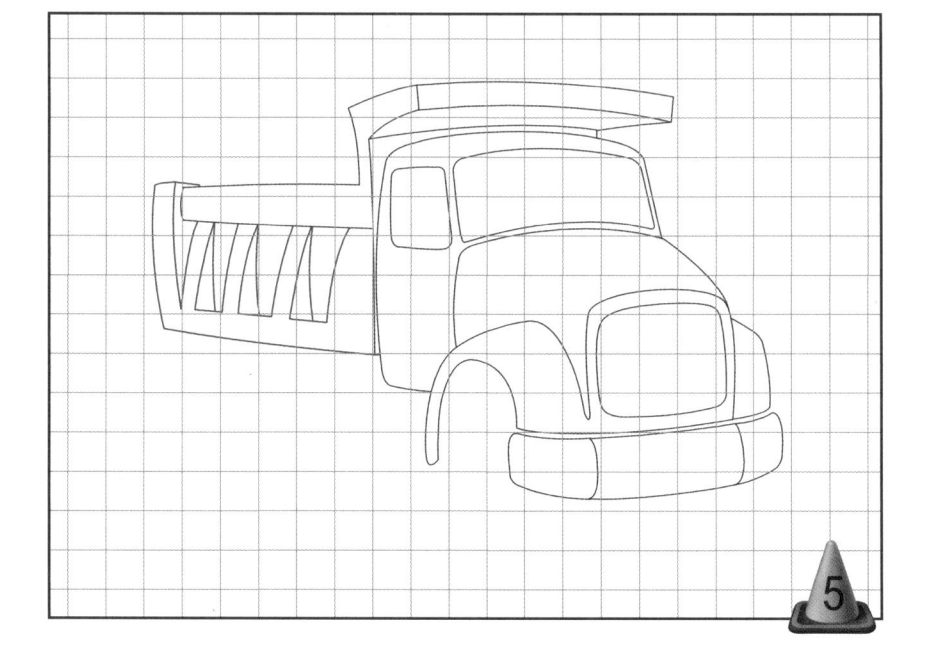

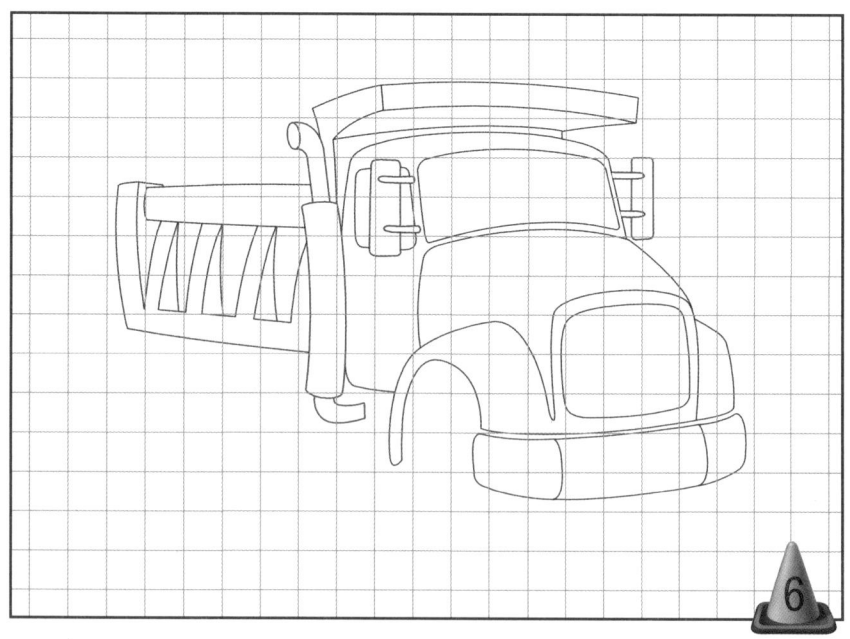

6 Draw two rectangular side mirrors, with two narrow rectangles for each to attach the mirrors to the cab. Draw the long, slightly curved rectangle for the muffler; add the pipe that attaches the muffler to under the cab, along with the exhaust pipe at the top.

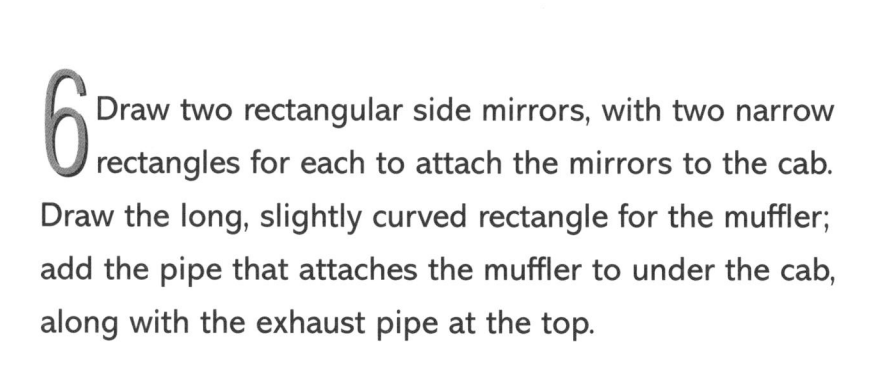

7 Draw three large ovals for the tires. Inside each oval, draw two smaller ovals, one inside the other. (Note: The ovals inside the back tires are closer together than the ovals inside the front tire.) Draw the rectangular step under the door; be sure to draw the short line that connects the step to the cab.

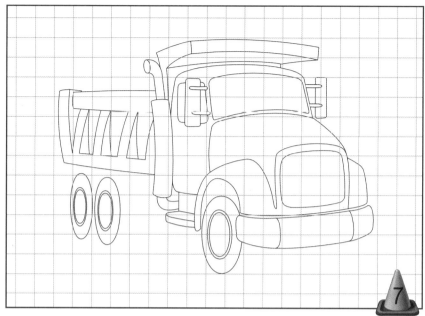

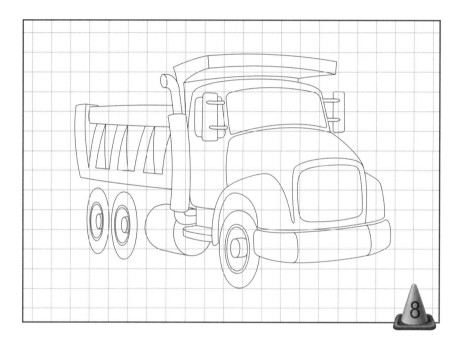

8 Draw a hub inside each tire. Draw the gas tank, which is a rounded shape with a circle at one end.

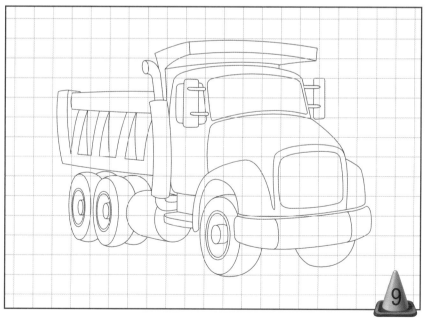

9 A dump truck has to haul heavy loads of rock and dirt, so it needs lots of tires. Make the tires look real by adding lines to create depth. Then add the second set of rear tires. Draw the front side tire under the bumper on the right.

10 Now you are ready to add fun details. Draw and outline two squares for the headlights. Draw another two squares for the lights in the bumper. Draw a square with a rounded corner behind the rear tires for the mud flap. Use your ruler to draw straight lines inside the grill. Draw lots of tiny circles all around the muffler, and draw four cab lights above the windshield.

11 Use a felt-tip pen to trace over the lines you want to keep, and erase the extra pencil lines. You can draw a dump truck!

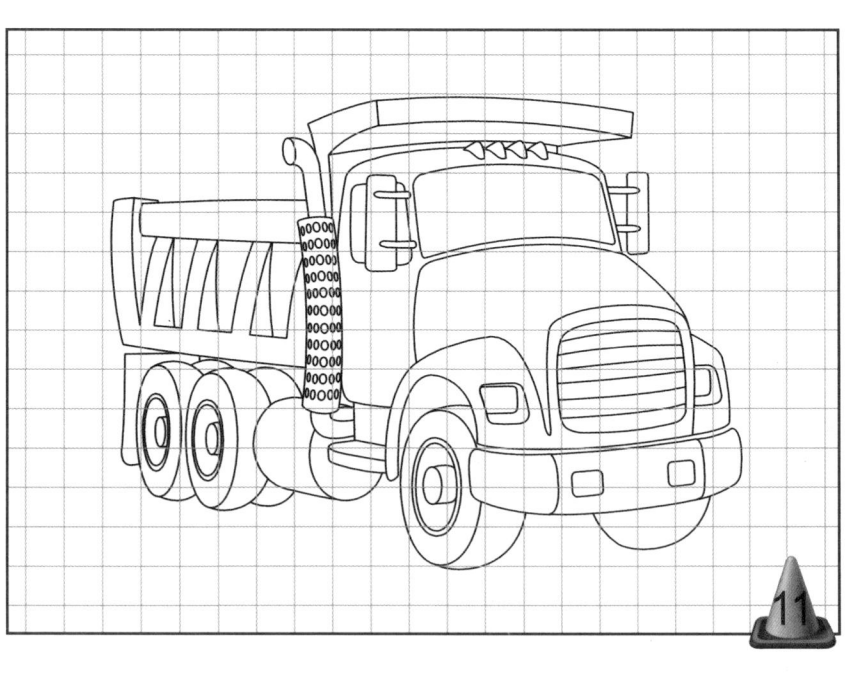

Earth Drill

The earth drill is a huge machine. It has a drill bit that spins in the ground to make deep holes in the earth.

1 Draw the shapes that make up the cab, hood, and frame of the machine. Note that the cab and hood sit on top of the frame.

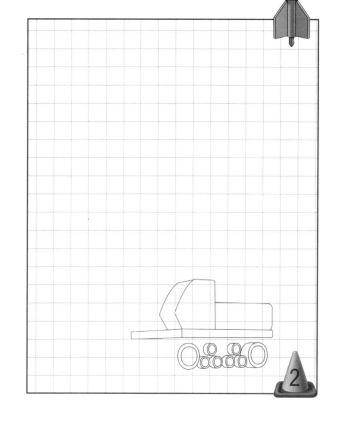

2 An earth drill is very heavy and has to travel over rough ground, so it needs long tracks. Draw all the wheels, adding outlines where shown to create depth.

47

3 To make the track, draw a line around all the wheels; draw another line just outside the first one. Add the outline to the front to create the face of the track. Under the platform and beside the track, draw the lines that make up the underside of the frame. Draw two narrow rectangles on the side of the hood. Draw two front windows and two side windows on the cab.

4 Draw a rectangle that covers most of the wheels inside the track; draw another rectangle around the first. For the tracks on the far side of the drill, draw all the parts that can be seen. To draw the extra-long boom, make a long rectangular shape that tapers at either end. Draw the triangles inside the middle of the rectangular shape—use a ruler to get the lines even. Draw the shape at the top of the boom.

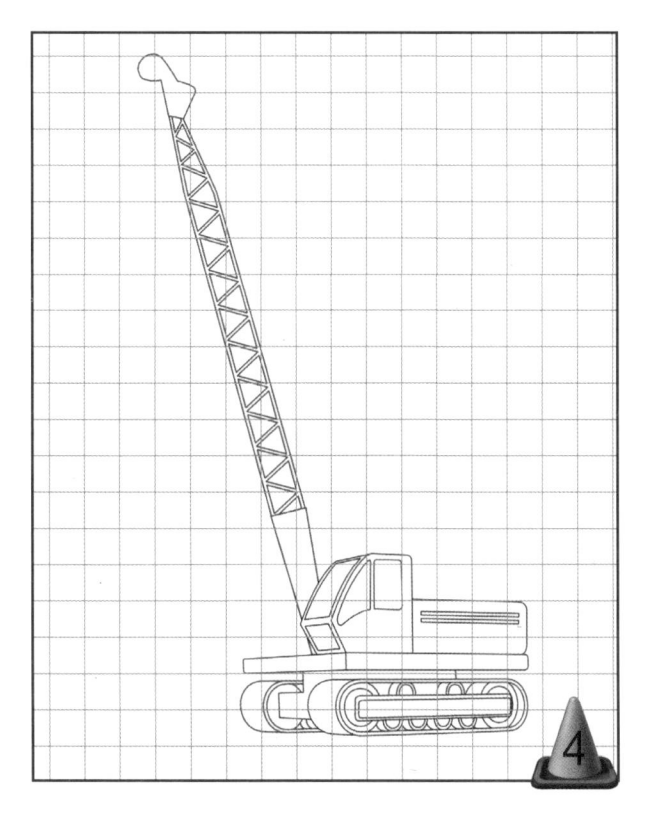

5 Draw the front of the boom; again, use your ruler to make the triangles. Draw a square at the base of the boom on top of the frame.

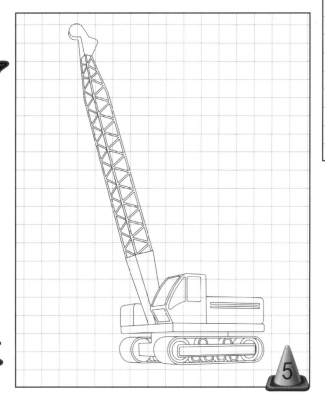

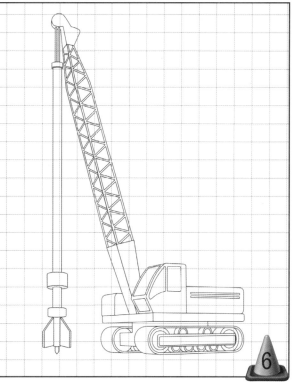

6 For the drill, draw a rectangle that is almost as long as the boom. Connect this rectangle to the top of the boom by two very thin rectangles for cables. Add the cuff to the top of the rectangle, just below the cables. Draw two more cufflike structures, one at the bottom of the rectangle and another a little above the first. Below the bottom cuff, draw the drill bit. At the very bottom, add the pointed shape.

7 Draw and outline the thin triangle shape that connects the drill to the boom; this is called the "moonbeam"—it holds the drill shaft steady. Behind the cab, draw the boom's cable guides. Notice how the top is rounded.

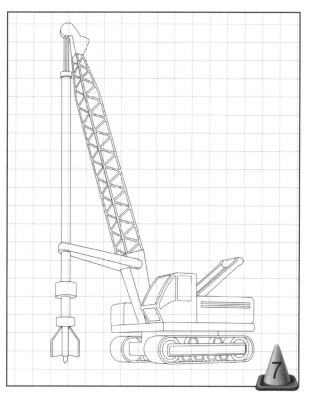

49

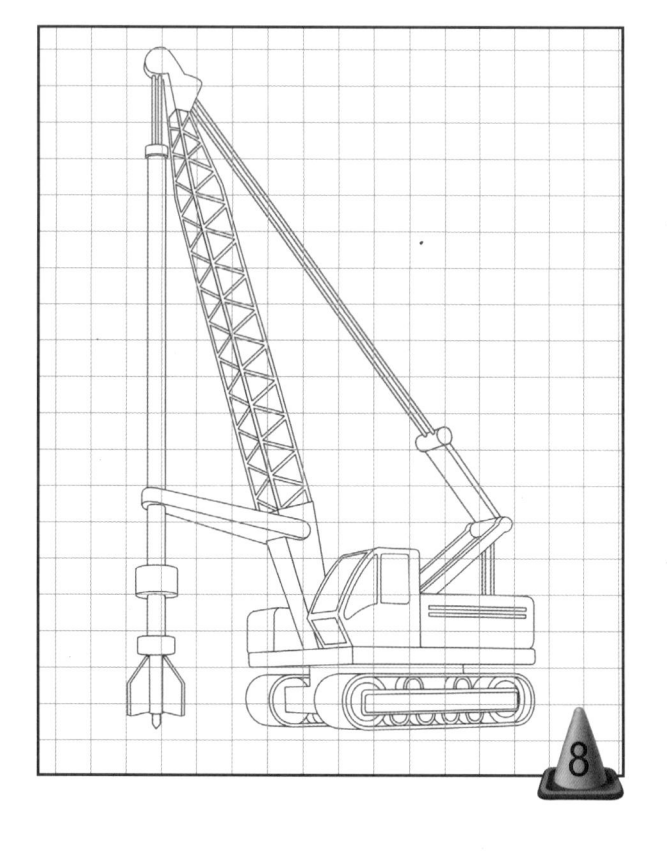

8 Draw and outline a rectangle above the cable guides. At the top, draw a rounded rectangle with a circle at the end. Draw two thin cables. Don't forget to extend the cables under the cable guide to the hood.

9 Use your ruler to draw tread on the tracks. Draw a safety light on the top of the cab. Draw a curved tube from the moonbeam to the base of the boom.

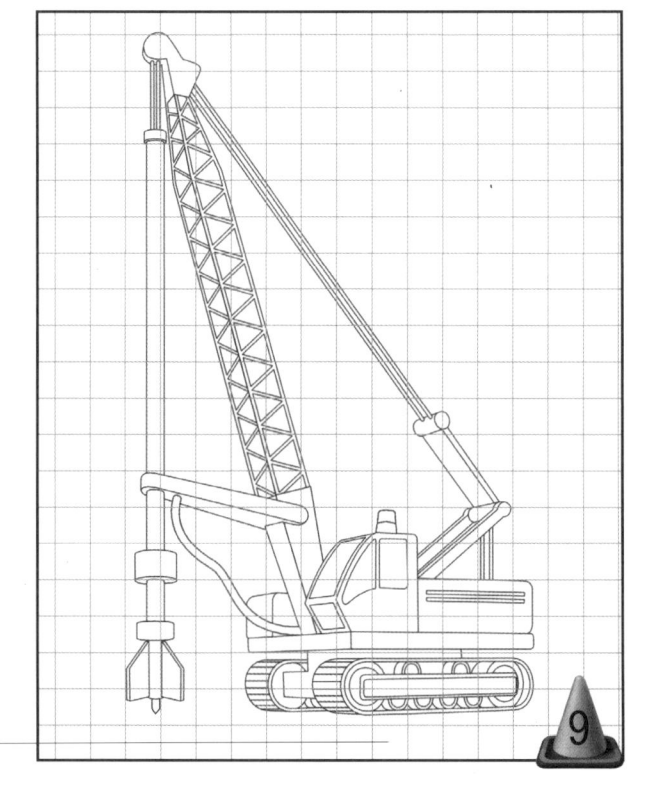

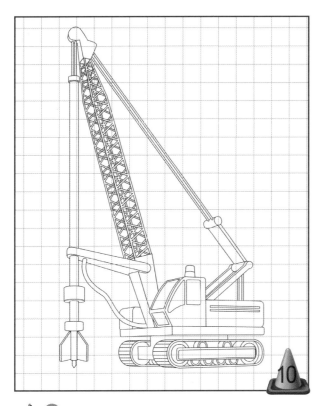

10 Now it's time to draw the back of the boom. Pay close attention to what you see when you are drawing. Look through the triangles you have already drawn to draw the back triangles—again, use your ruler to make this job easier.

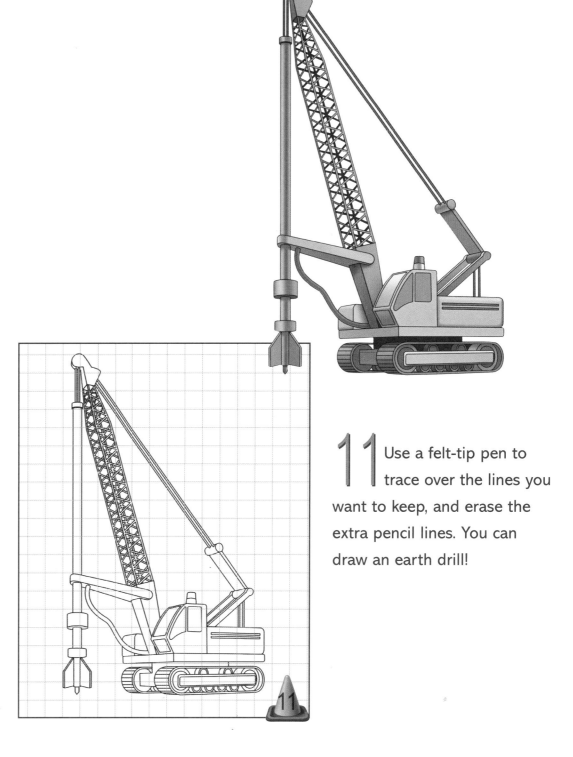

11 Use a felt-tip pen to trace over the lines you want to keep, and erase the extra pencil lines. You can draw an earth drill!

Elevating Conveyor

An elevating conveyor is a powerful machine used to scrape up topsoil.

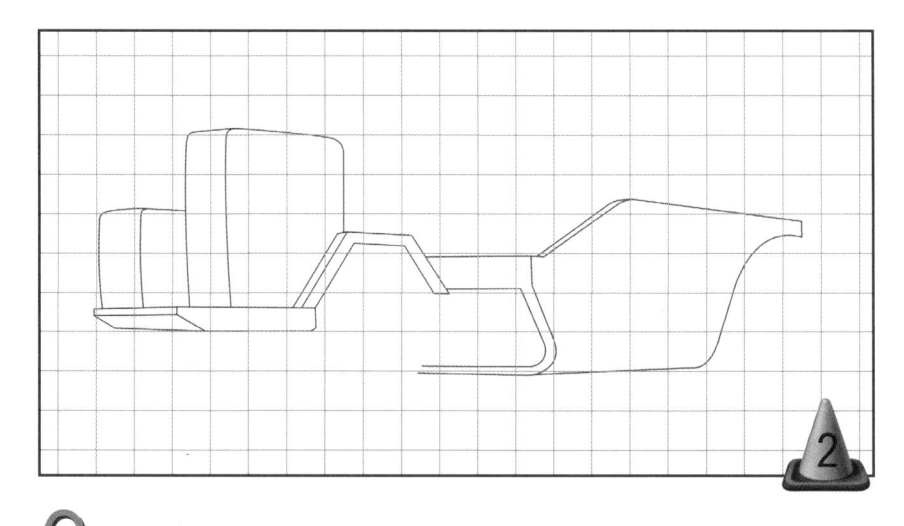

1 Start by drawing the shapes for the cab, fender, and front bumper.

2 Near the cab, draw a square to make the hood; add a vertical line to create a cube shape. Toward the rear is the big drag pan. Look at all the lines, and copy what you see.

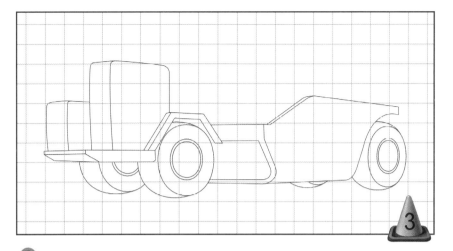

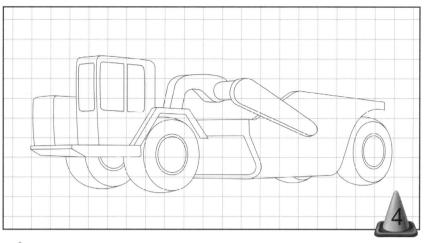

3 Draw the wheels. Each one looks a bit different because of the angle of the machine on the page. Draw what you can see.

4 Add three windows in the cab—notice how some corners are curved but some are square. Next draw the drag pan hitch, which looks like a big lever. Outline the shapes to create depth.

5 Draw a muffler above the hood. The muffler is a rectangle with a pipe running through it. At the front of the hood, draw a rectangle, adding horizontal lines, for the grille. Draw the hubs inside the side wheels. Add lines to create depth to the center of the wheels.

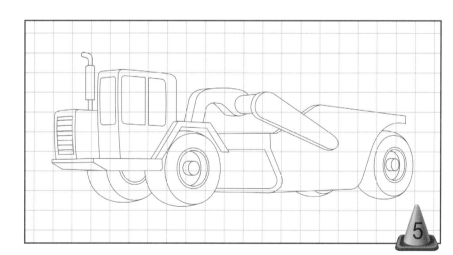

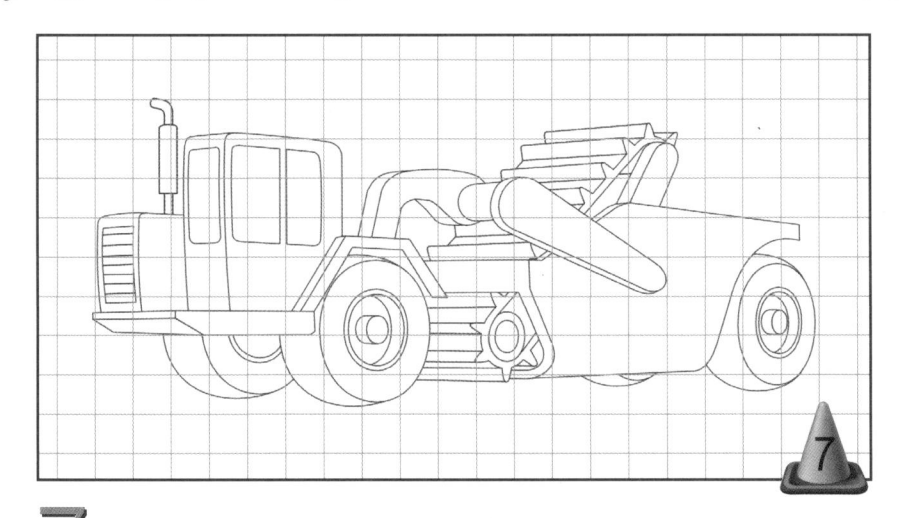

6 The conveyor seems complicated, but you can do it! Draw a ring behind the front tire. Above the drag pan, outline a rounded rectangular shape. Connect the ring and rectangle by a loop. Draw another loop around the first, adding small, evenly spaced triangles all around it. There are two other small lines that you need to draw in—one is inside the loop at the top and the other is behind the handle of the lever.

7 Draw horizontal lines that start at the triangles you just drew. Use a ruler to keep your lines straight. Notice how these lines make up the conveyor belt. On the far side of the belt, draw small lines to connect each of the triangular shapes to each other.

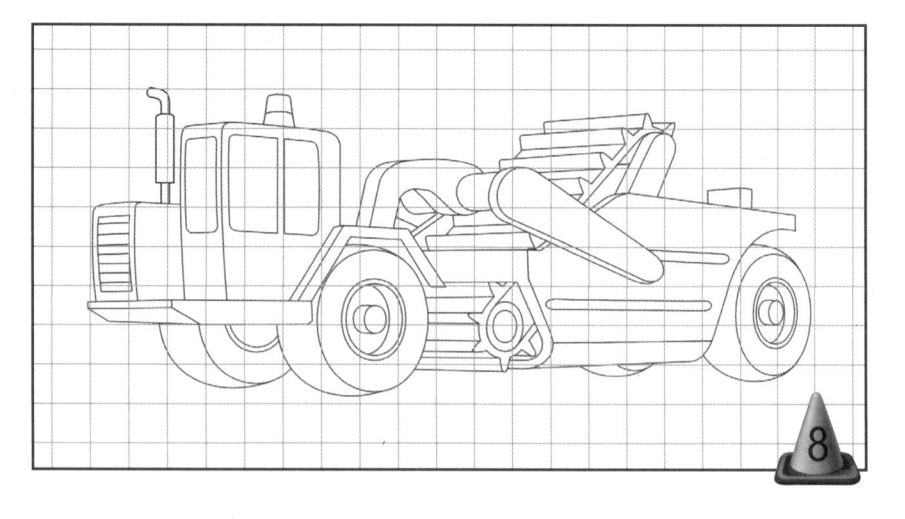

8 Finish the body of the machine by drawing a safety light on top of the cab. Draw other finishing details, including ridges on the side of the pan and a square on the pan's back deck above the rear tire. Draw the lines that complete the lever and other side of the machine.

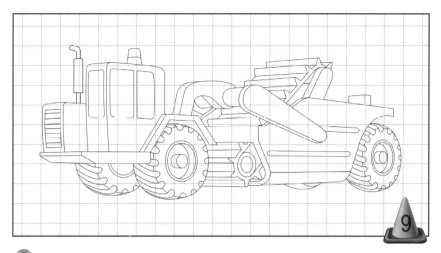

9 Add tread to the tires. The tread is made up of evenly spaced diagonal lines. These lines come together at a rounded end on the outside of the tire.

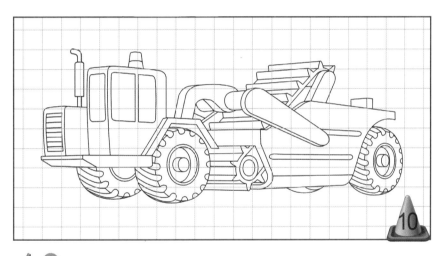

10 Use a felt-tip pen to trace over the lines you want to keep, and erase the extra pencil lines. You can draw an elevating conveyor!

Grader

A grader is used to make roads. It can flatten and even out nearly any rough surface.

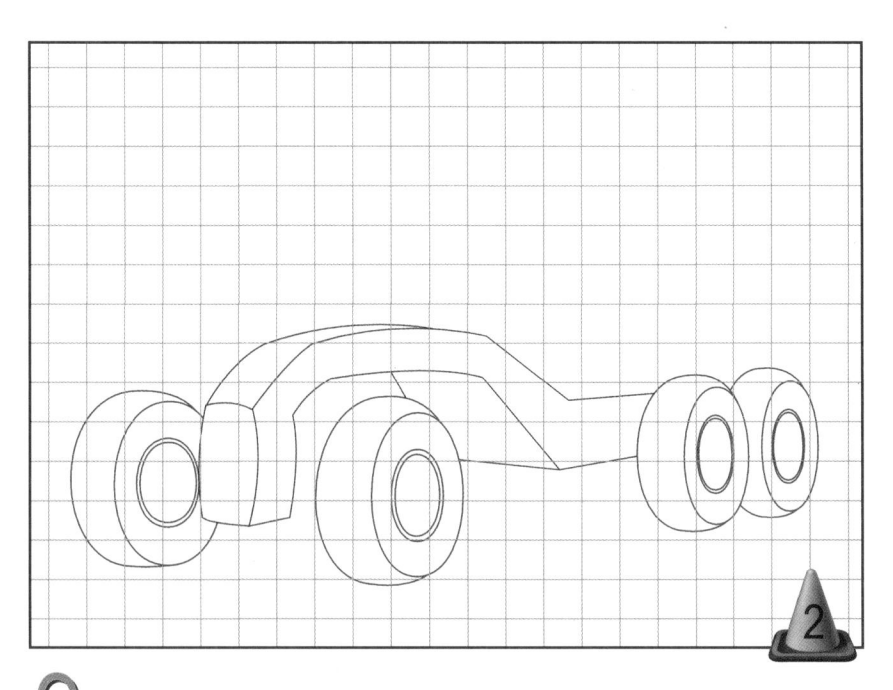

1 Begin your drawing with a shape that looks like a sideways question mark. Add depth to the shape by adding the corresponding lines.

2 Draw two front tires and two rear tires. Add the two circles inside each tire to make rings, and add lines to create depth on the tires.

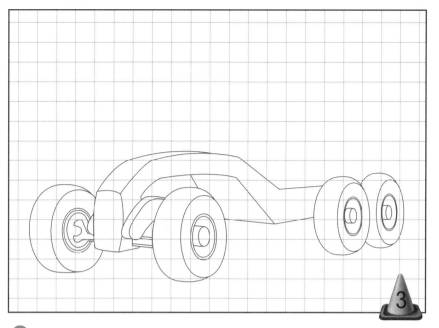

3 Draw the hubs inside each wheel facing you. Draw all the details that make up the front axle. This area looks complicated, but draw what you see.

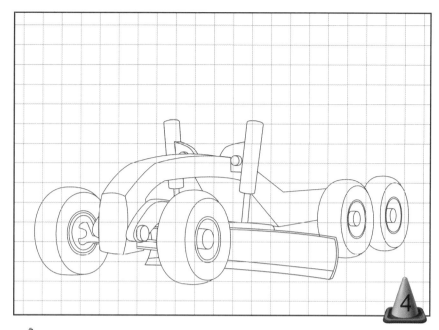

4 Draw a long, slightly curved rectangle for the grading blade—some of it is hidden behind the front wheel. Draw the cylinders that attach the blade to the frame of the grader. Add the brackets that attach the cylinders to the grader frame. Add all the large bolts, including outlines for depth.

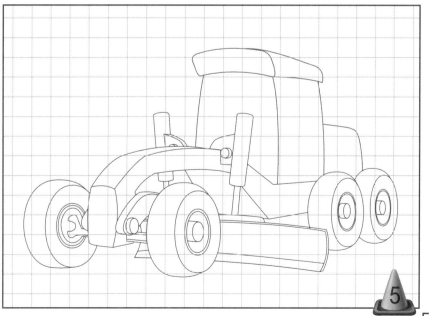

5 To make the cab, draw two large rectangles. Add a slightly curved rectangle to the top of the front of the cab and a smaller rectangular shape behind it to make the roof. Draw a small square with rounded corners behind the cab for the engine hood.

6 Draw the squares and rectangles that make up the windshield and side windows. Draw two sets of circles in the front of the roof for lights. Near the front rear tire, draw a rectangle with a square in front of it for a step.

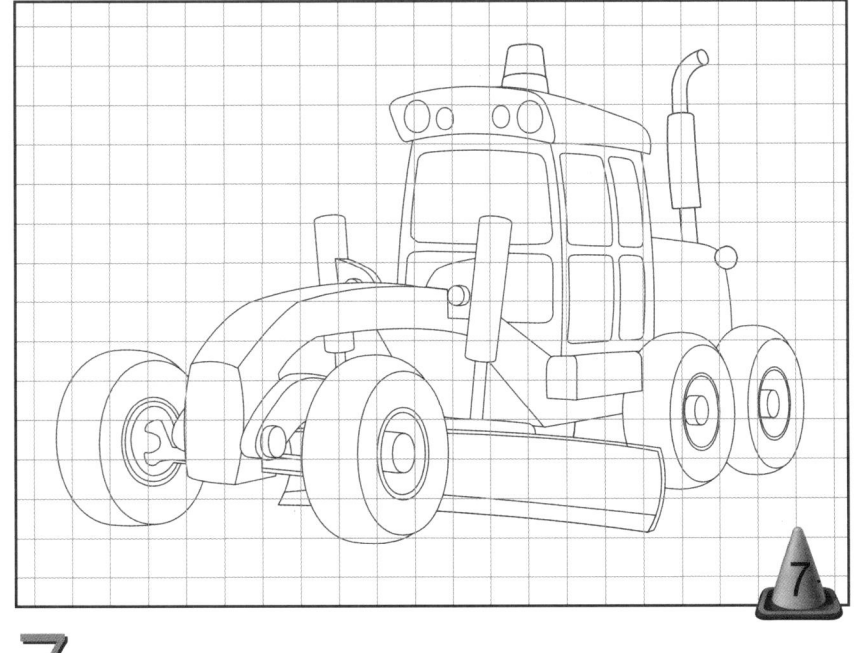

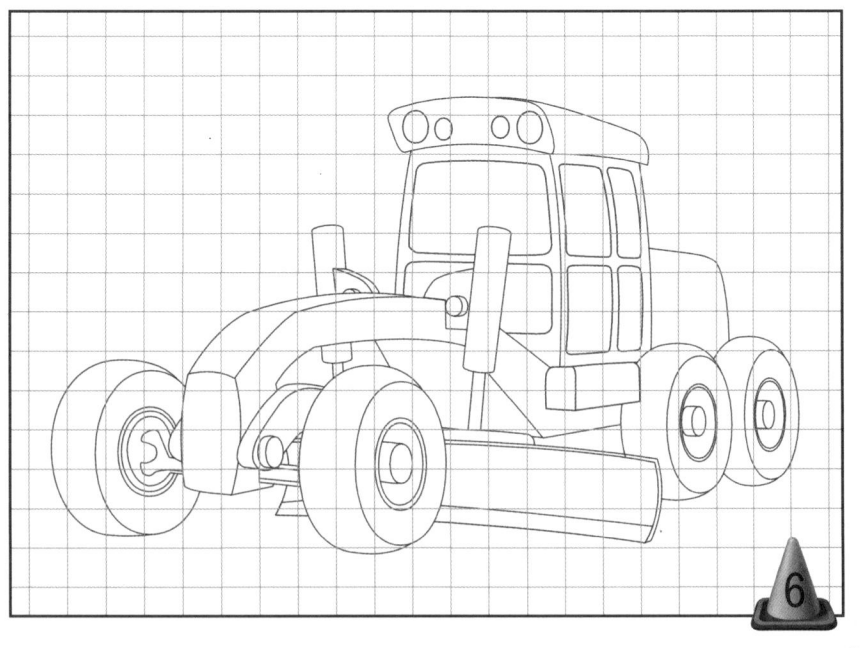

7 Add a safety light on the cab's roof. Draw the muffler, which is a slightly curved rectangle with a pipe running through it. Draw the back of the taillight at the rear corner of the engine hood. Draw the line for the rear tire on the far side of the vehicle.

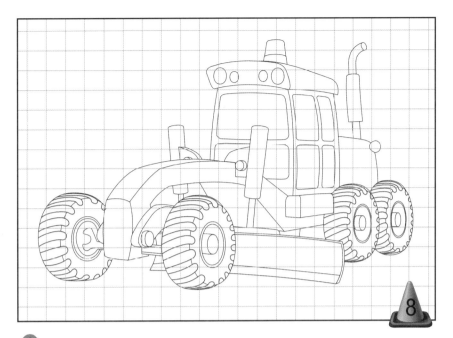

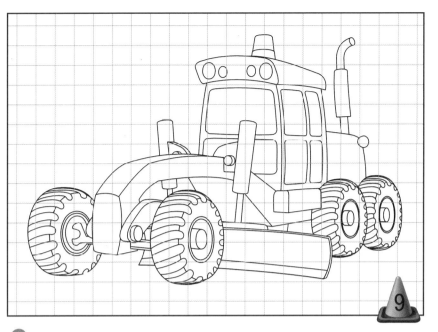

8 Draw tread on all the tires by making evenly spaced diagonal lines that come together at the rounded end on the the outside of the tires.

9 Use a felt-tip pen to trace over the lines you want to keep, and erase the extra pencil lines. You can draw a grader!

Backhoe

The backhoe is a versatile machine—it can dig and scoop with its buckets on the front and back.

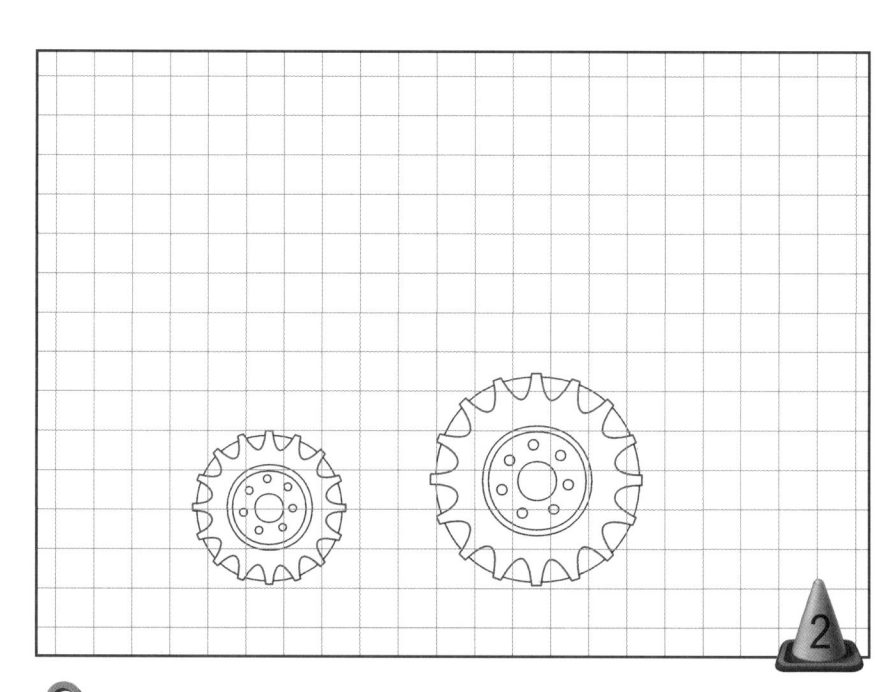

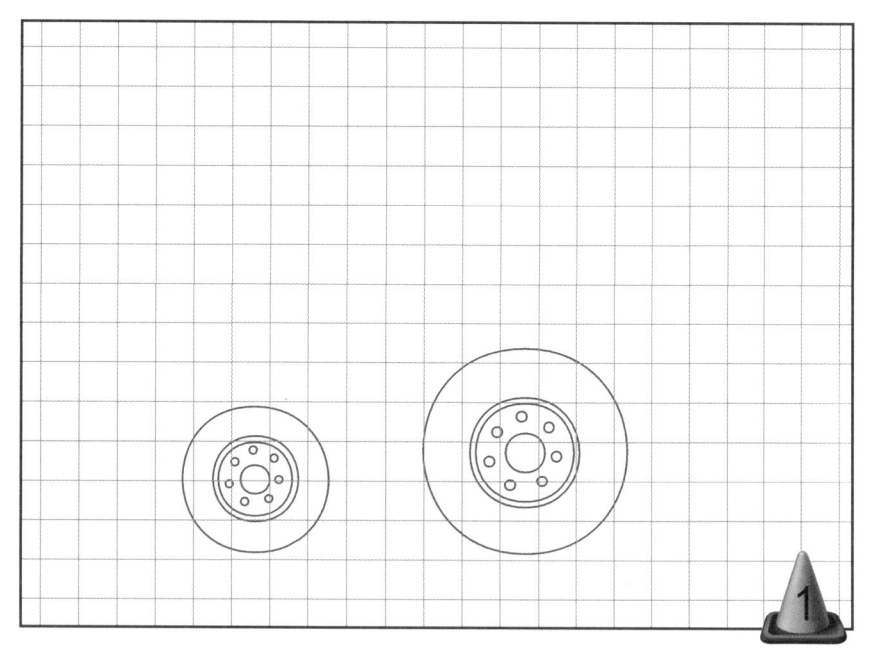

1 Begin by drawing the wheels, which are made up of many circles.

2 To add tread to the tires, draw a series of half-ovals, connected by a small straight line, around each of the outside circles. This is fun to do!

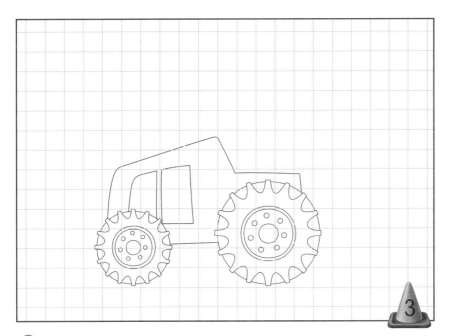

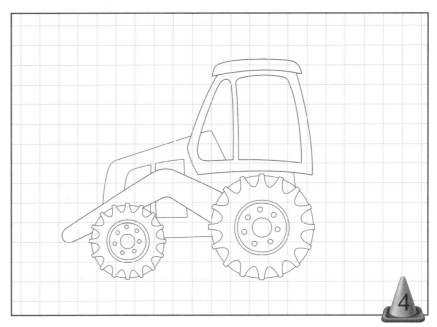

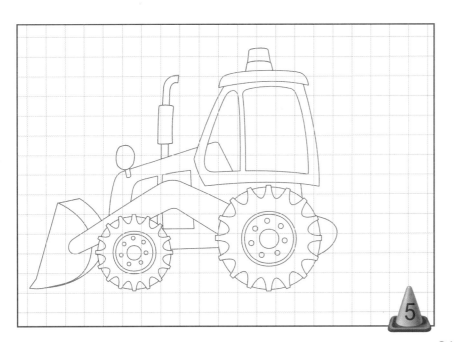

3 Draw the shape that makes up the body of the backhoe. Draw two rectangles inside the front of this shape. Be sure to round the one corner as shown.

4 Draw the cab; notice how the top of the shape is narrower than the bottom. Draw the windows in the cab. Draw the roof. To the side, draw a sideways L shape from the back wheel to past the front wheel. The end of the L is rounded.

5 Draw the safety light on the cab roof, and draw the back of the headlight at the front of the hood. On the hood, draw the muffler, which is a rectangle with a pipe running through it. For the front bucket, draw a half circle, adding a point at the bottom. Add the line to create the front of the bucket. Outline bucket to add depth. At the rear, draw a small bump behind the tire.

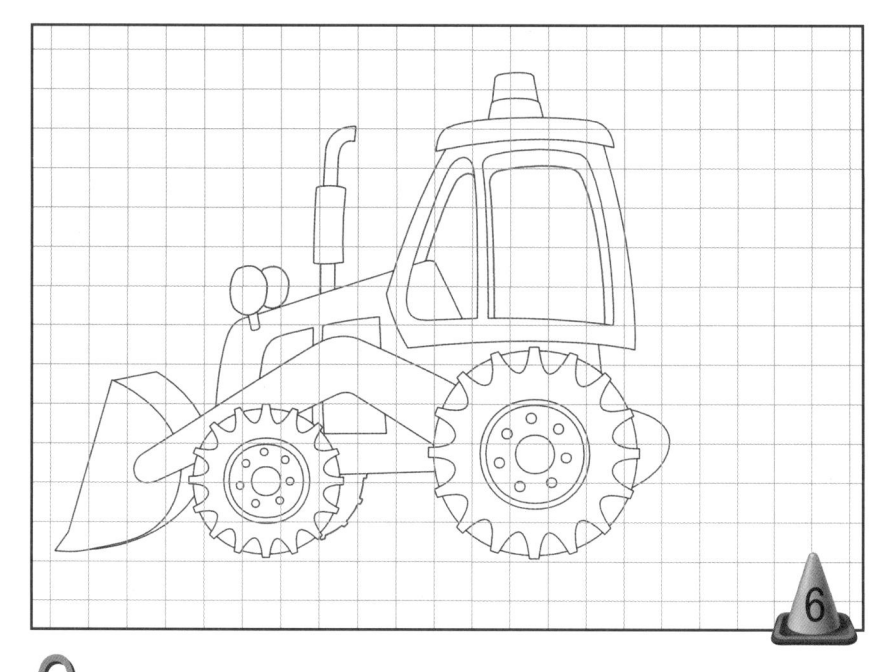

6 Draw all the details on the far side of the backhoe that you can see from this side, including the other headlight, the windows on the other side of the cab, and the edge of the front tire on the far side. Look carefully at the pattern the tread makes.

7 Draw the arm for the backhoe scoop. It is made up of two curved rectangular shapes with rounded ends. Outline each rectangle for depth. Draw the rounded triangular shape on the lower arm.

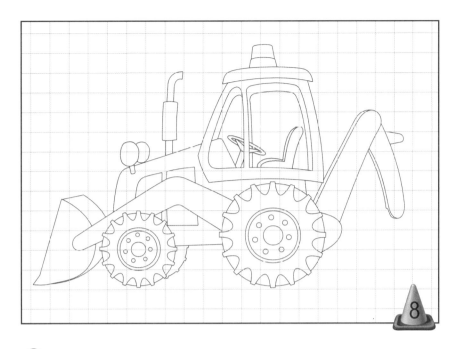

8 Draw the steering wheel and driver's seat inside the cab. Add detail lines for depth.

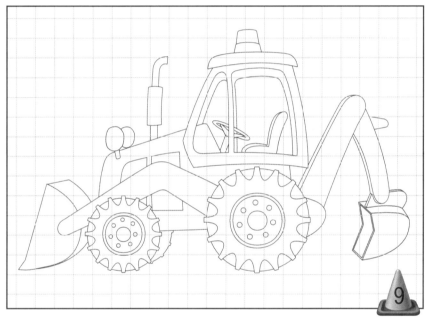

9 Draw the backhoe scoop. Look at the example to see how it attaches to the boom.

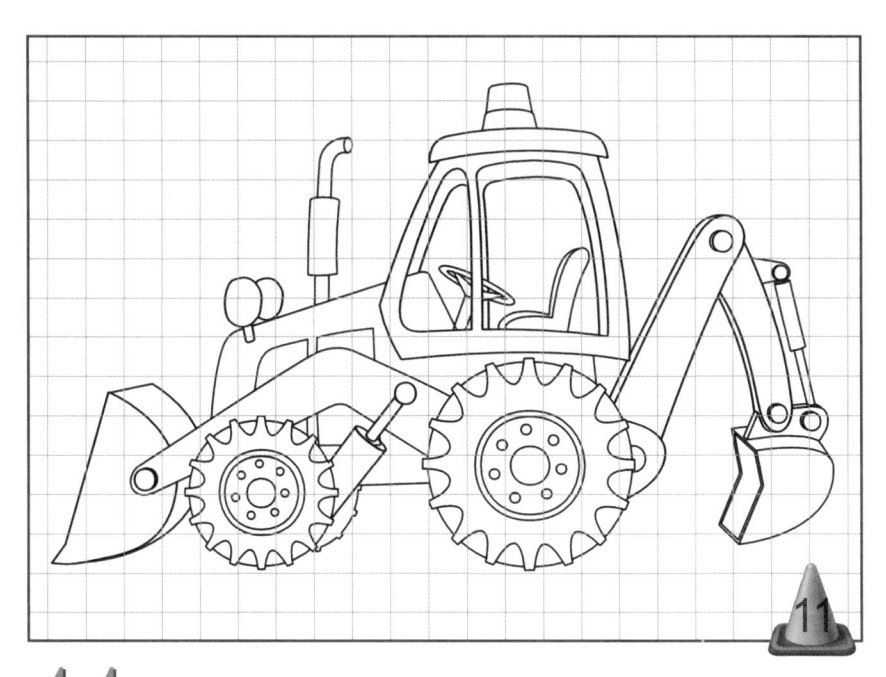

10 Add all the circles for the pivot points that move the arms up and down. Outline the circles where indicated to add depth. To finish your backhoe, draw two hydraulic cylinders.

11 Use a felt-tip pen to trace over the lines you want to keep, and erase the extra pencil lines. You can draw a backhoe!

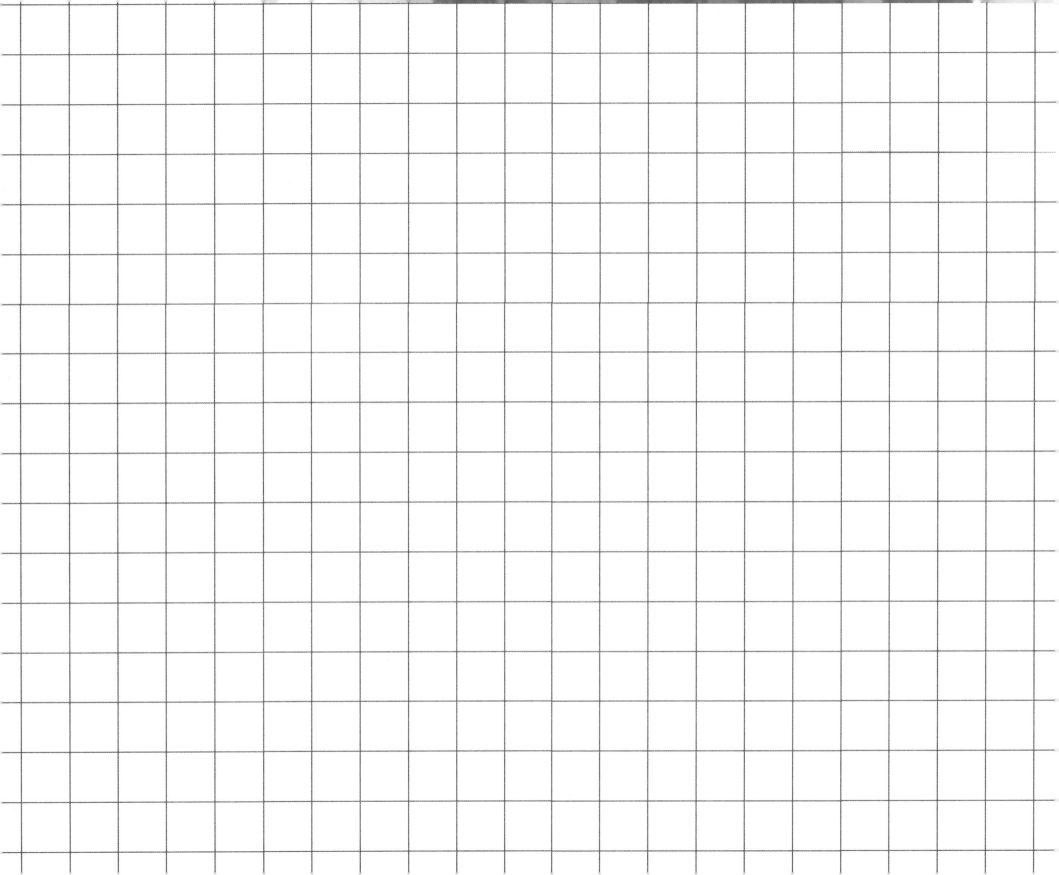

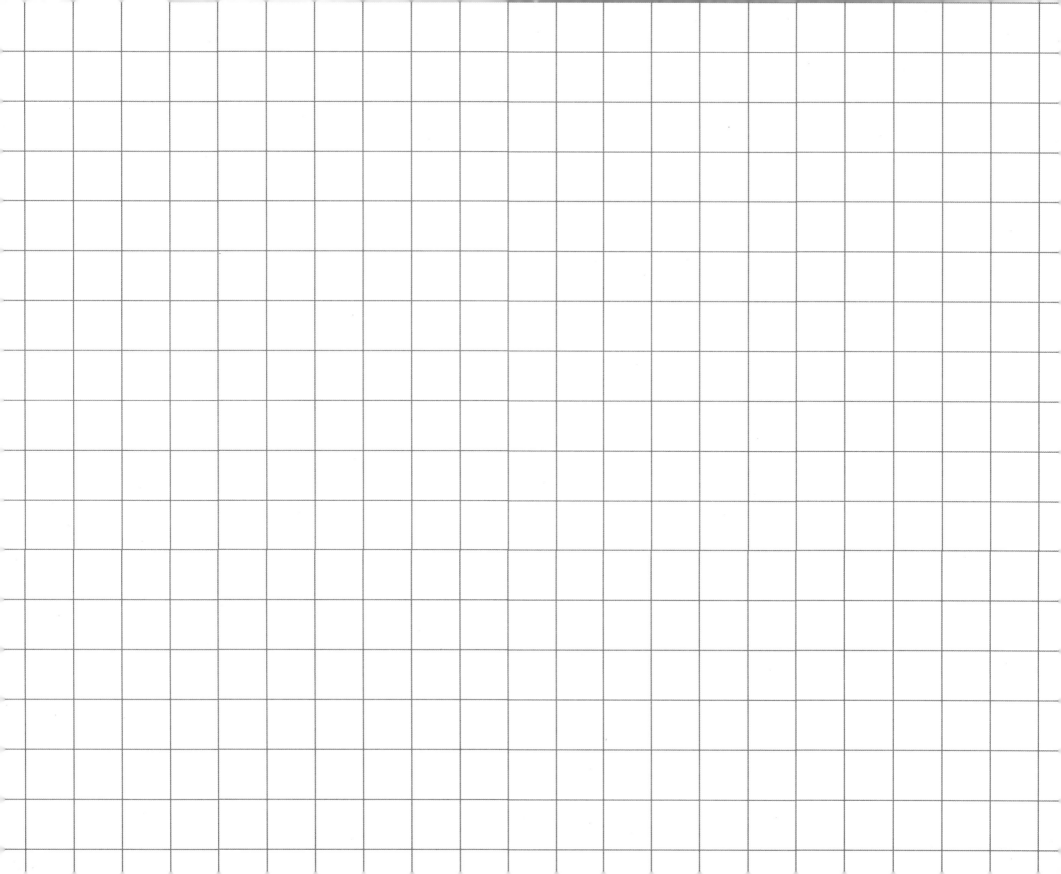

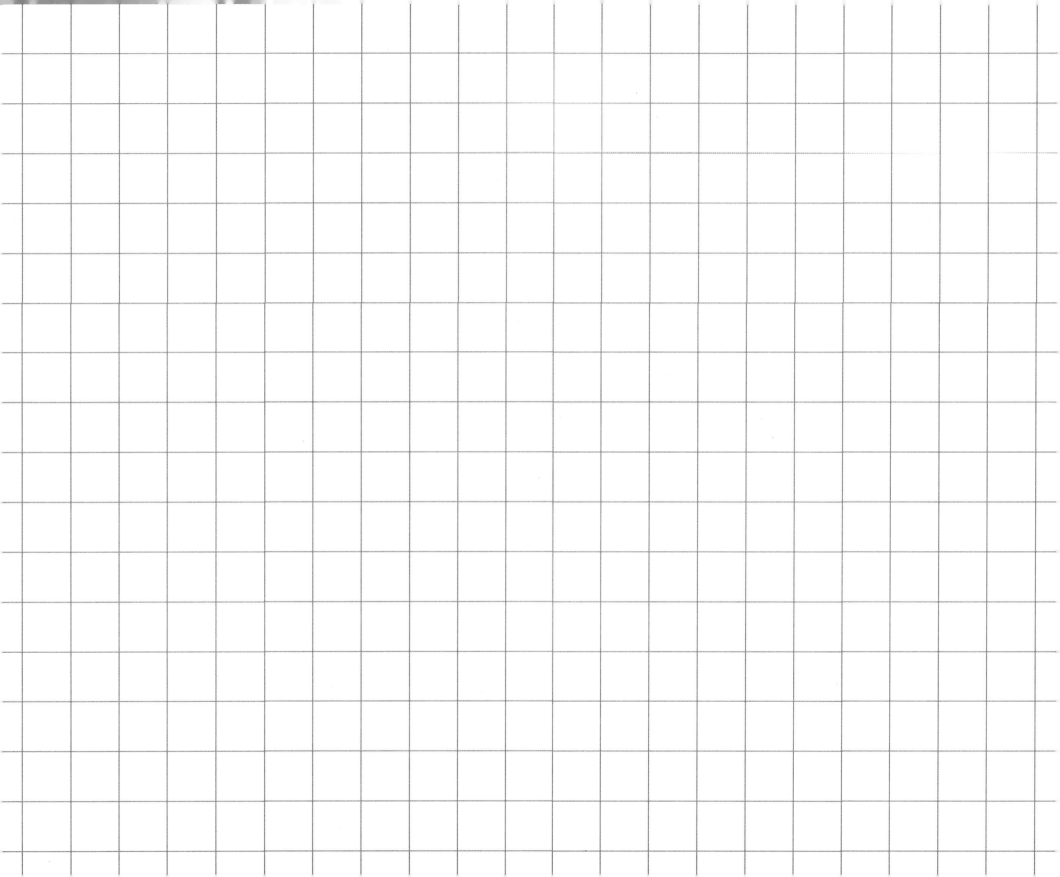

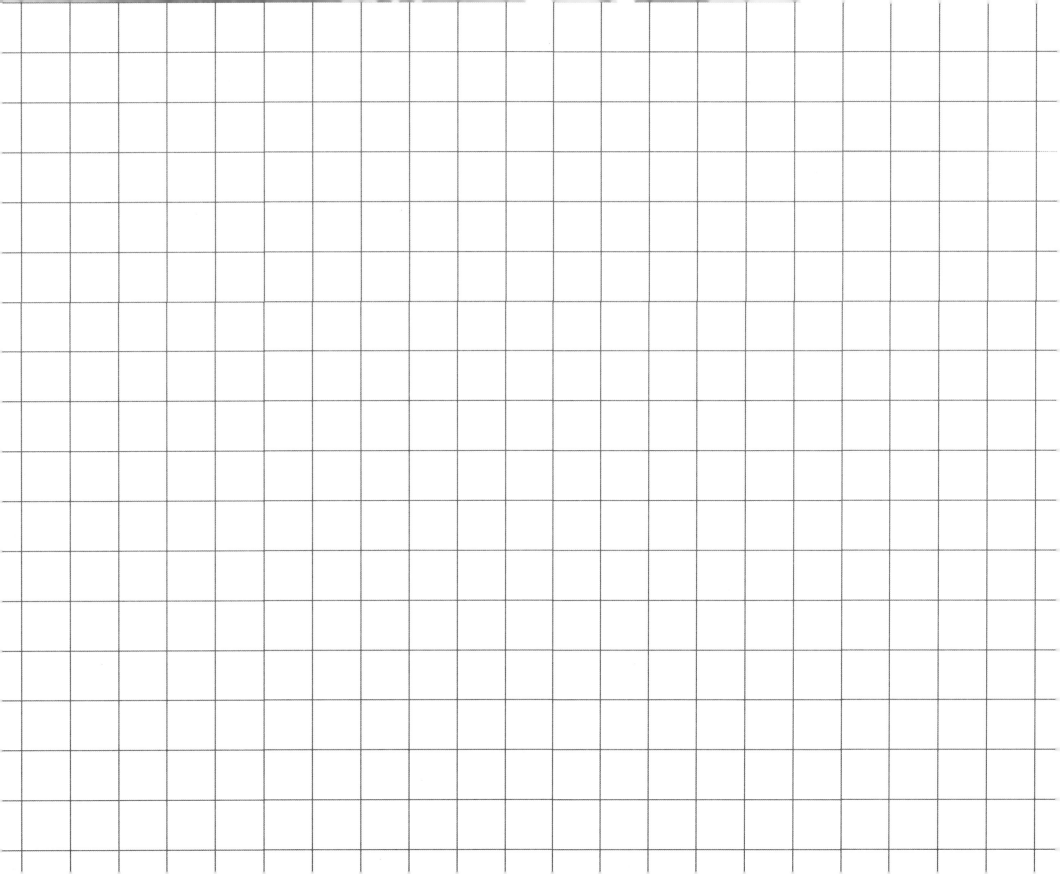

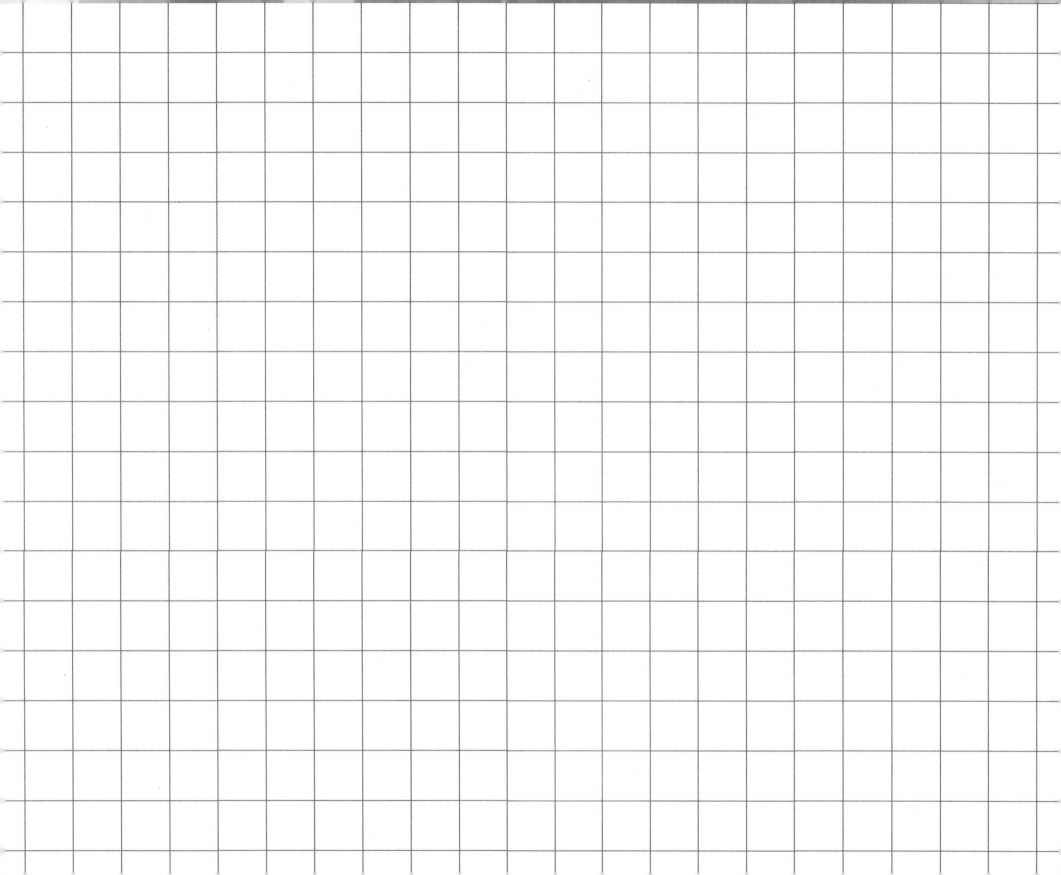

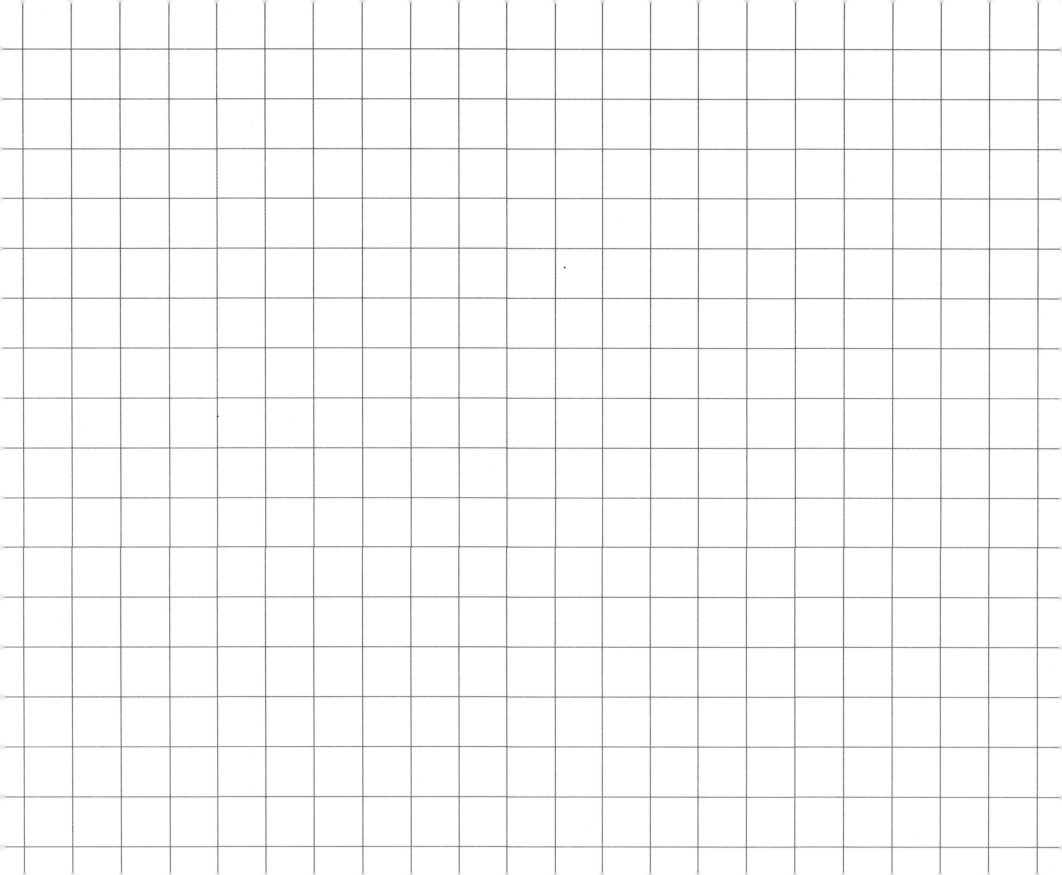

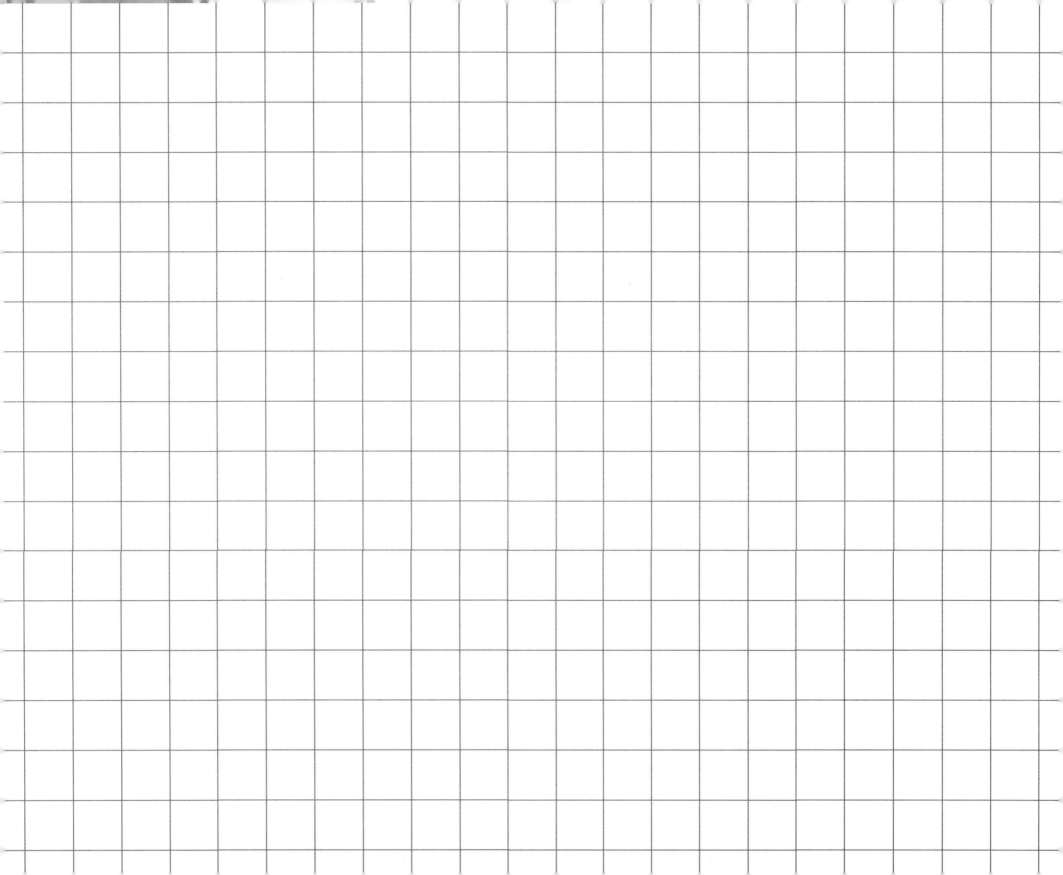

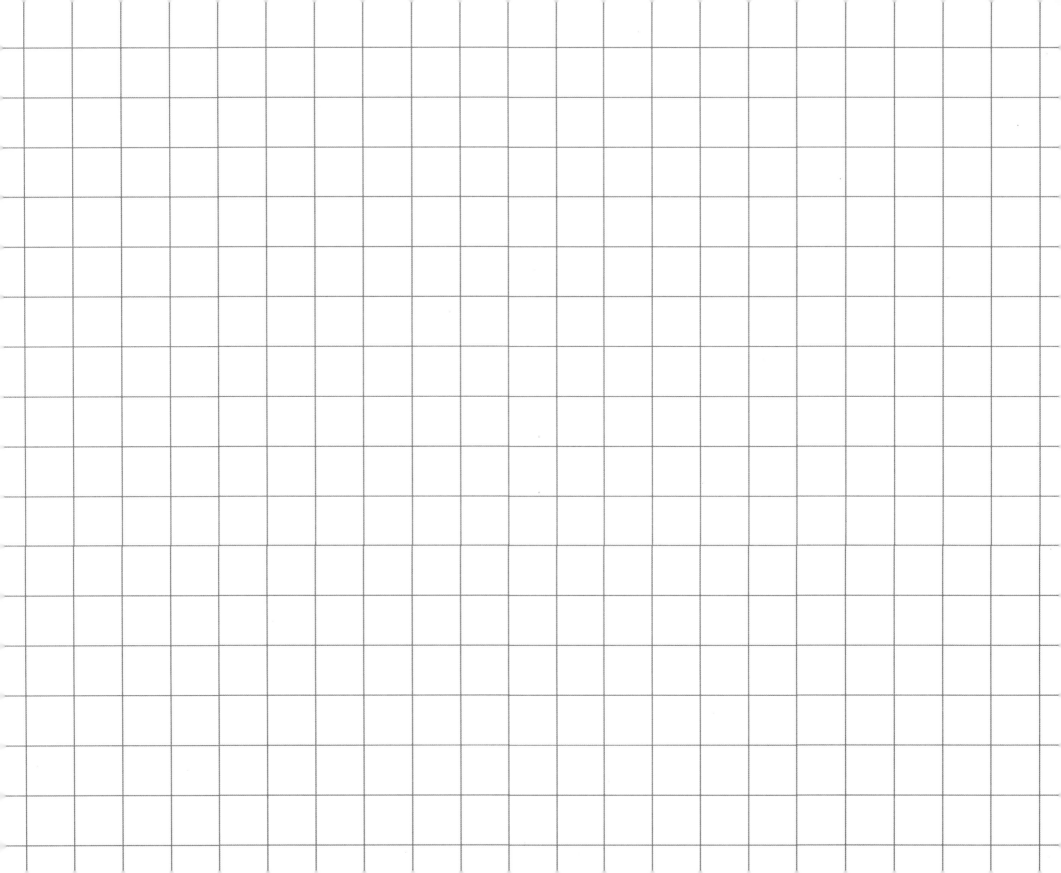

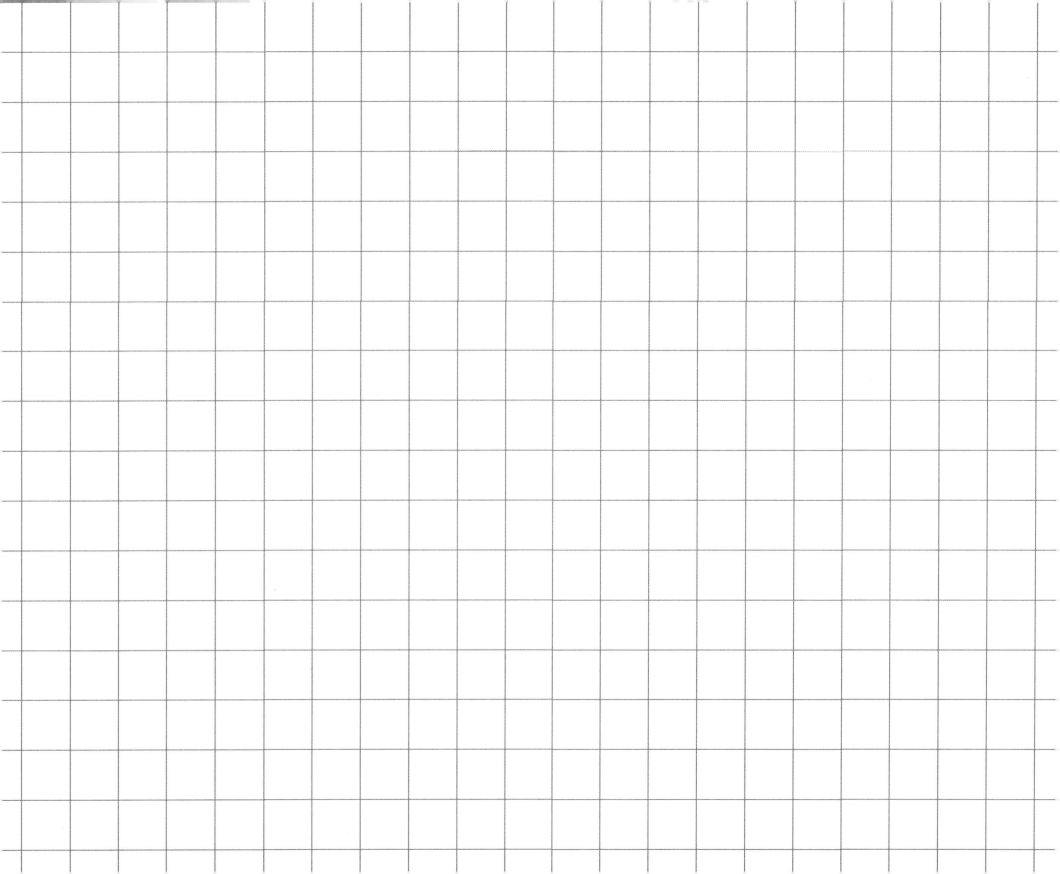

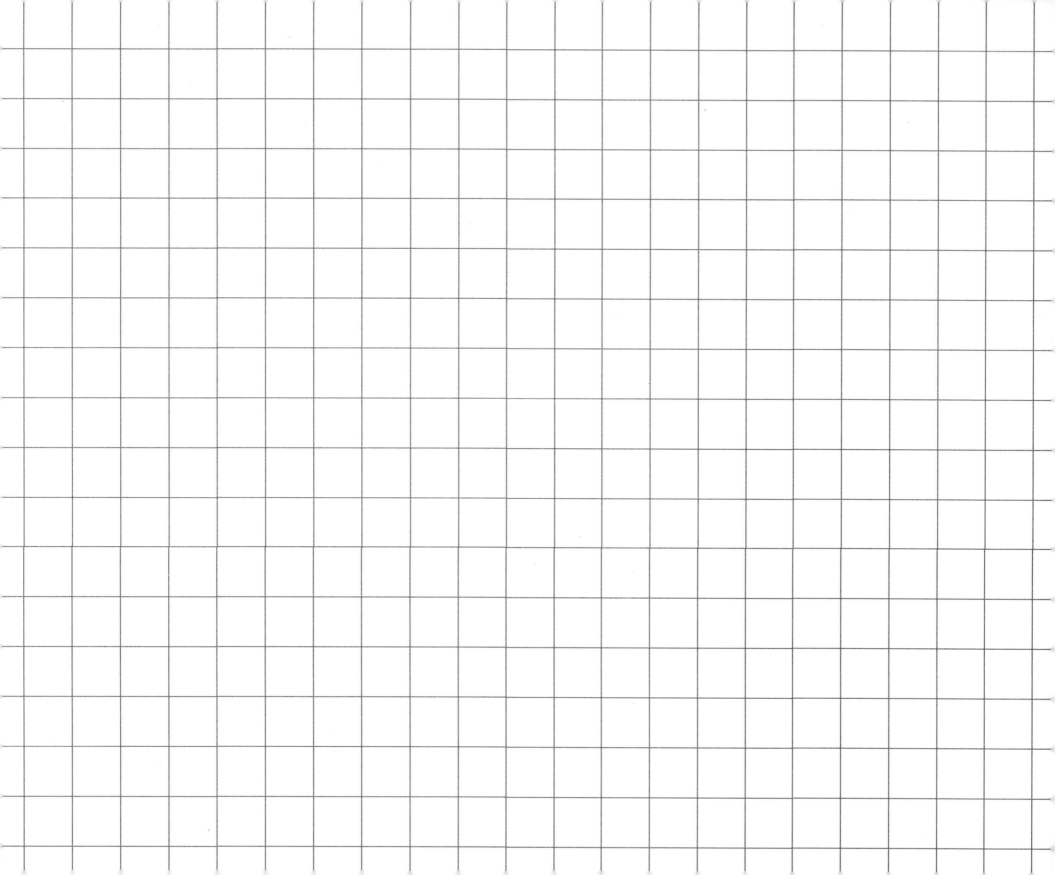

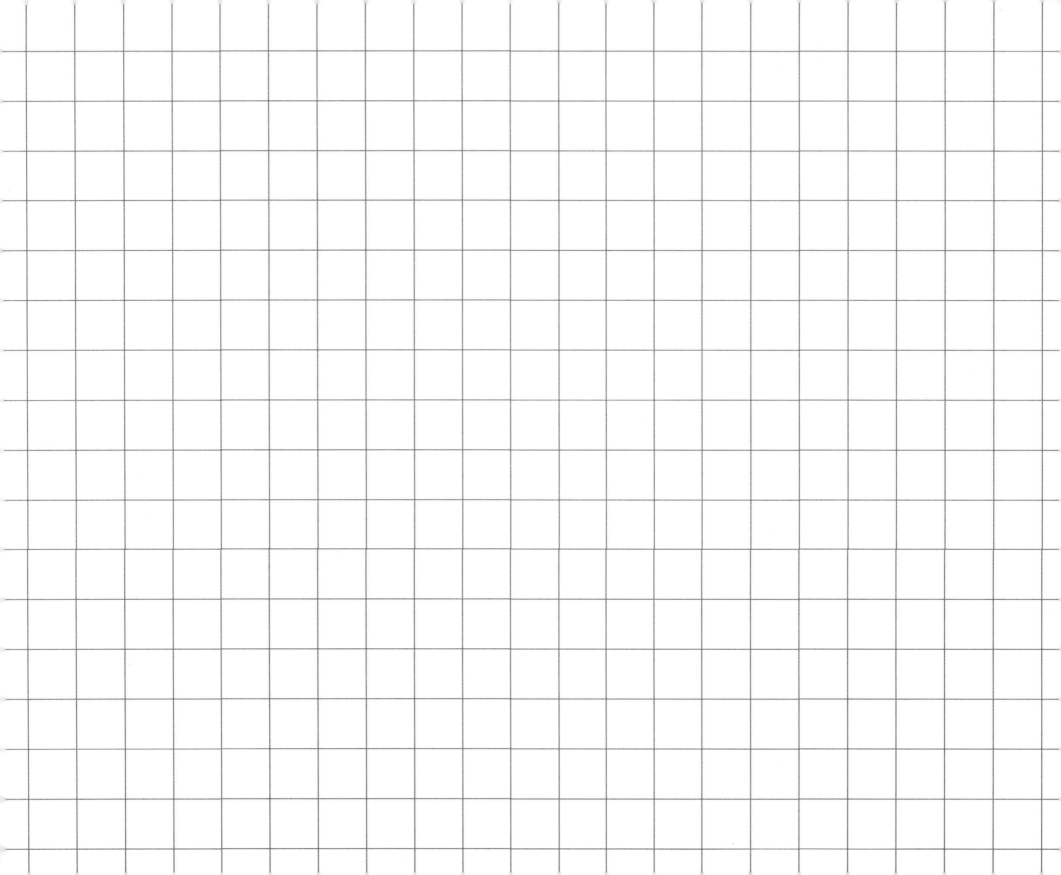

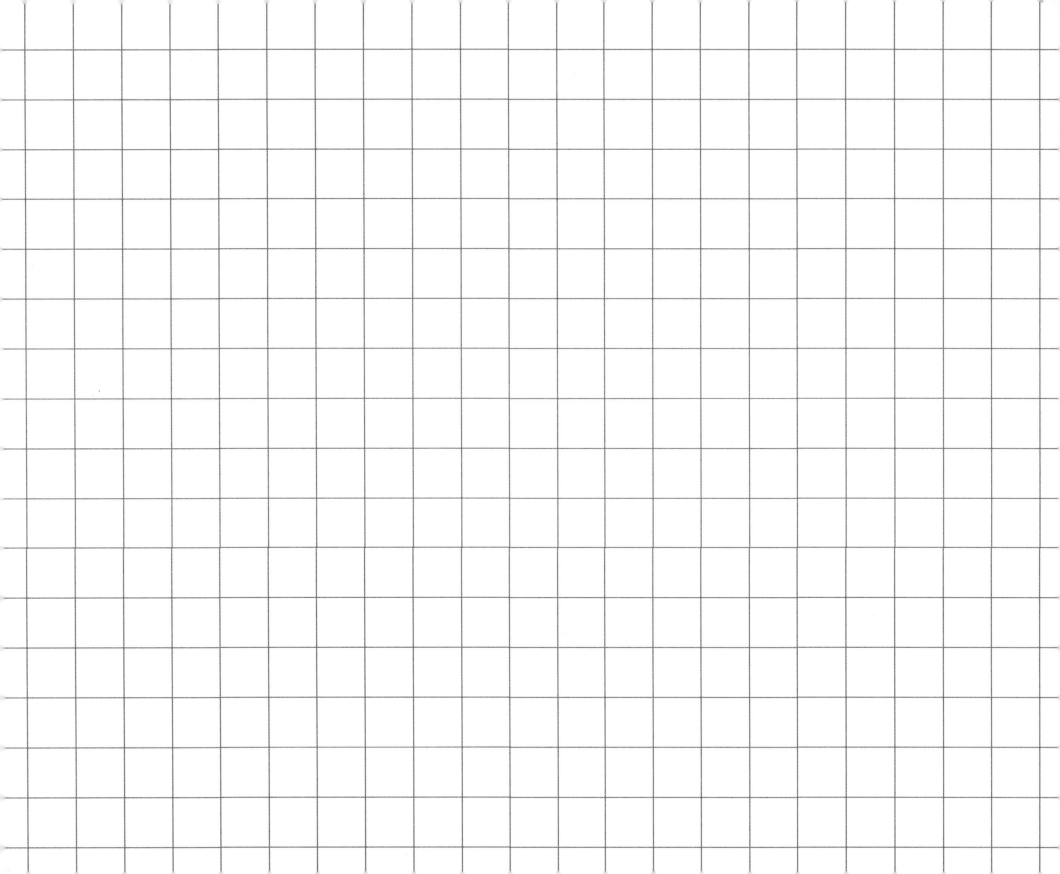